STORM JIN-ZARI

02-19-10

Dear
Rinku dixit c̄ Family.
c̄ best complimts
from Author.
[illegible]

STORM JIN-ZARI

Love Story

Chloe Production Films,
Hansa Mahendra Shah

AuthorHouse™
1663 Liberty Drive
Bloomington, IN 47403
www.authorhouse.com
Phone: 1-800-839-8640

Storm Jin-Zari
Novel, Movie Drama
Love Story
By
Hansa Mahendra Shah, RN

July 18th 2008

This is a work of Fiction. All of the characters, organizations, and events portrayed in this book are either products of the author's imagination or are used fictitiously.

First published by AuthorHouse 11/12/2009

ISBN: 978-1-4389-7624-2 (e)
ISBN: 978-1-4389-7623-5 (sc)

Library of Congress Control Number: 2009911986

Printed in the United States of America
Bloomington, Indiana

This book is printed on acid-free paper.

Storm Jin-Zari

Love Story

Story & Screenplay by

Hansa Mahendra Shah

"Live & Let Live"

In Memory of
My Late Brother
Pradeep Mohanlal Jobanputra

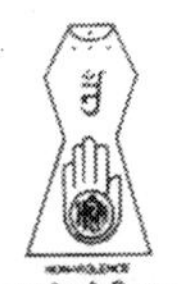

JAINA

Federation of Jain Associations in North America

Founded 1981

A Non-Profit Tax Exempt Religious Organization IRS Code Section 501(c) (3) EI # 54-1280028

NGO in Special Consultative Status with the Economic and Social Council of the United Nations

JAINA Headquarters: 43-11 Ithaca Street, Elmhurst, NY 11373 USA: Phone & Fax (718) 606-2885

May 18, 2008

Dear Hansaben:

It was indeed a privilege and honor to read manuscript of your upcoming book STORM: JIN-ZARI.

Your story of repentance and redemption is a deeply moving one that every immigrant to America can relate to. What impressed me most was the essence of Jain principles woven into storyline. You have touched on present day issues of immigrant society with dash of interfaith marriages and struggles of new generation as they traverse two different cultures. Twists and turns of the storyline draw the reader into turning pages after pages to see where the characters end up. All the main characters of the story are worthy of our attention and admiration.

I would like to see the manuscript result in a published book and later into a movie for the benefit of all who believe in the essential goodness of human spirit.

Sincerely,

Dilip V. Shah

Dilip V. Shah
President
JAINA

Samarpan Jain Sangh, Inc.
(A Non-Profit Organization of Delaware Valley)
9701 Bustleton Avenue
Philadelphia, PA 19115
Telephone: 215-464-7676 • Telecopier: 215-677-9919

November 17, 2008

Mrs. Hansa Shah
1696 Powderhorn Drive
Newtown, PA 18940

Subject: Manuscript

Dear Hansaben and Mahendrabhai,

I have read your manuscript. It is the same I think, as you had shown me last time with some changes. It is obvious that you are very keen to have it published or to have it turned into a movie. If you are persuaded that you have a talented director and are willing to give him the freedom, I think he can turn it into a good movie.

With the election of Obama we have discovered that America is changing. There may be great curiosity about different cultures, philosophies and ways of life. With the ecomomy facing difficulties, my guess is that it may be possible to have a wide choice of independent filmmakers whom you can join to implement your ideas.

I wish you good luck. I appreciate you giving me an opportunity to read your script. You are so enthusiastic and creative. Meeta sends regards.

Yours sincerely,

Devendra T. Peer

DTP/bmk
enclosure

Subject: Requestion permission for Jain Material in "JinZari-STORM" book
Date: 3/31/09 4:07:02 AM Eastern Standard Time
From: vinod@kapashi.wanadoo.co.uk
To: Hansaphytherapy@aol.com
CC: mukeshkapashi@rediffmail.com
Sent from the Internet (Details)

To,
Hansa M. Shah
President
Chloe Production Films, LLC

Re: Permission for using Jain Material in Storm Jin-Zari Love Story, book

Dear Hansaben,

I was pleased to know that you have undertaken a project of publishing a book called Storm Jin-Zari Love Story. This sounds quite exciting and our best wishes are with you. You are, at this instance, are allowed to use material from our Jain University's web-site. Please ensure that you acknowledge Jain University.org at every possible step. Good luck.

Vinod Kapashi
Mukesh Kapashi

ACKNOWLEDGEMENT

Thanks to the following persons, They are: Dr. Mahendra Shah, Dr. Hiren & Dr. Malathi Shah, Dr. Nilesh & Usha Rana, Mr. Bipin & Neeta Jobanputra, Mr. Vinod & Mukesh Kapashi (UK), www.JainUniversity.org, Mr. Dilip & Sarla Shah, Mr. Devendra & Dr. Meeta Peer, Mr. Girish & Vimla Gupta, Mr. Rashmi & Bhavna Kamdar & Mr. & Mrs. Pravin Shah ("Times" Studio Mumbai, India) & J. J. Vrajdham Haveli (Ahmedabad, India)

Contents

Part 1

OPENING SCENE

OUTDOOR SCENE (Create the climax of suspense) Empty deserted street as heavy rainfalls, the droning of thunder and lightening on the deserted road...

Front car lights blaze in the darkness. Close up the car wipers flicking to and from as the girl tries to start the car. Camera from outside captures the face of a young beautiful woman, large eyes seated inside the car.

Fair-skinned young modern woman Zarina a Christian in her mid twenties is dressed in a beige pantsuit and boots. Rain suddenly comes to a stop. Her eyes moved to read the sign 250th Street & Broadway - The car has stopped in front of a lonely deserted bar.

A sudden crack of thunder as Zarina pushes the car door open and rushes to see what is wrong with the car, she tries ... and tries to open the hood, before she knows what is happening - three shadowy figures stand around her. She looks up, terrified, it is still drizzling and everyone is soaking wet. Shadows of three men come out on the street. They looked like they have been drinking. The leader drinks last drop from the bottle and smashes the glass on the pavement.

ZARINA: (Terrified, but trying to stay calm and unnerved) *"Please, do you think you can help me? It may be, the clutch ... starter is not working... or may be the alternator?"*

LEADER: (Shadowy rough guy in the darkness ... no close-ups) *"Help? Hey guys, this beautiful hot babe needs our help..."*

SECOND GUY: (Hoarse laughter mimicking in a girlish voice) *"Help, help, help..."*

THIRD GUY: (Comes out of the dark shadows he has cold eyes) *"You look so different from our girls.... Where did you come from?"*

ZARINA: (Tries to keep her cool, showing she is not afraid but she is petrified -) *"I think I have a flat tire..."*

LEADER: (Stands close next to Zarina) *"Flat? ... Flat tire ... Speak American ... what kind of language is flat tire?"*

ZARINA: (Tried not to show the fear ... but her eyes start showing it) *"Flat tire"* (Turning and pointing to the wheel of the car)

LEADER: (He approaches her and grabs her arm ... she screams) *"Don't be stupid sister, we need to have some fun ... and here you are ...ready for the fix..."*

ZARINA: (Starts to run and drops her car keys on the road. She stops turn around. But the Leader moves in his drunken state and picks up the keys, jingling and then swinging it into the air. As Zarina moves towards him to get her keys back, he throws it to the next guy and then the third guy jingles the keys.)*"Please, I need the keys to get home ... please!"*

LEADER: (Drunk and playfully repeating her please, extending his hand to give her the keys) *"Please, please ... Hey guys, it's not nice to make a beautiful dame beg..."*

Zarina stands facing the Leader, and without hesitating, she tries to grasp the keys, and finds herself in the Leader's arms. Next moment, he tries to kiss her. Without a moment of hesitation, Zarina struggles out of his grasp and slaps him across the face with all her strength...

LEADER: (Surprised at her sudden action, his hand on his face, he punches her and she falls to the Ground) *"You bitch ... I'll teach you a lesson tonight. Nobody messes with me, and gets away with it, you whore..."*

(Shouts aloud)

From nowhere, a black Harley Davidson motorbike appears front light glowing in the darkness, spotlighting the scene on Zarina lying on the road and the Leader ready to start raping her, as a knife sparkles in the night. He moves towards her. Next moment, the rider puts the bike on a louder high gear and swings halting between the two. He starts the bike and moves recklessly noticing the two other guys walking towards him. He swings on his loudly roaring motorbike and drives towards them instantly; they are both seen running. The Rider than put the bike in reverse and swings back towards the Leader and breaks in front of him.

JINEN SHETH: (Tough loud voice, warning the Leader ... He is outraged by the attack on the girl) *"I have called the* *cops on the cell phone and they will be here any minute ... If you value your life, you will leave immediately ... or spend the rest of your life in jail..."*

LEADER: *"Where the hell did you come from? This is none of your business ... Who the hell are you ... you crazy bastard? You Mama's boy ... Go back from where you came from ... before I change my mind and beat the life out of you..."* (Knife glitters in the darkness) *"I can cut you both up into shreds..."*

JINEN SHETH (puts his motorbike in full gear roaring his anger and the police car siren is heard around the corner) *"Get lost before the cops arrive ... You bully..."*

(He puts his hand out to Zarina, signaling her with his eyes to get behind the motorbike ... She moves swiftly towards him and they are seen driving off into the black night)

SCENE 2

Scene in Dunkin Donuts in midtown ... with motorbike parked outside ...

JINEN: (in front of counter)*"Two cups of coffee.."*

ZARINA CHRISTIAN:*"I would prefer hot chocolate, as I have had too much coffee at work today (*Pause) ... *I need to phone my father, but my cell phone is dead."*

JINEN: *"Why trouble him right now in your terrible state ... I can give you a ride home ... and tomorrow your people can go and pick your car up."*

ZARINA: *"No, no ... I must talk with my father ... Having been born and bred in this country, I can't understand how and why mere strangers ... have such violent thoughts in their minds ... I have to admit, I am quite shaken up thinking about the attack. I could have been raped. . I need my father to come and pick me up ... You have no idea how terrified I was ... But I refused to let them see it."*

JINEN: *"Now just relax. ... Sit down and settle your nerves ... I can understand what you're feeling. When I was in college, I was mixed up in a gang fight ... there are no winners and losers ... Just relax. I would never wish what happened to you on any friend of mine ... You were quite brave ... Don't worry your father..."*

ZARINA: *"Yes, I tried so hard to stay calm ... If you hadn't arrived ... I refuse to think what would have happened. In all that rain and thunder, passing through the street, my car just stalled. You were certainly God-sent ... I am grateful for you ... I can't think what would have happened ... Do you think my car will be safe out there?"*

JINEN: *"Here is a cup of hot chocolate ... just relax and sit down ... the rain was not helpful at all ... You can always buy a new car, but not a new you ... I dread thinking what they would have done ... That part of town is really rough - why were you driving in that place so late at night?"*

ZARINA: *"I left my Wall Street office and instead of taking the Westside highway, I thought driving through Harlem and then uptown would be less traffic ... Never again."*

JINEN: *"Where do you work at in Wall Street? I also have a job there at one of the major financial houses. I am a graduate* *from Wharton Business School in Philadelphia. That's where I was born and my family comes from."*

ZARINA: *"So you are in high finance too? I graduated from New York University with an MBA in business management and finance."*

JINEN: (Starting to joke...)*"Not many girls can tackle the economics of high finance ... It is not easy..."*

ZARINA: *"I had no trouble ... I was an A-student with a 4.0 average and a full scholarship ... My father is in business and I thought after some American business experience, I would manage his company ... Daddy has always encouraged me to read good books and go for higher studies ... Since I was 18, I accompanied him on his business trip to France, Germany, England and Sweden. I love to travel, experience new challenges, and meet new people. He always told me to follow my dreams - You can be whatever you want to be and do whatever you want to do ... So here I am working in a large American multinational company in high finance ... getting the right kind of experience..."*

JINEN: "*Oh, by the way, my name is JINEN SHETH. Here we are two complete strangers - talking about our lives, family matters and ambitions, and we don't even know each other's names. This is worse than a blind date.."*

ZARINA: *"Hi my name is Zarina Christian"*

JINEN: **"***Hello, Zarina Christian..."*

ZARINA: (Wondering with a look)*"Do you have a problem?*

JINEN: *"Oh, no ... no problem ... Zarina, it is a pleasure meeting you..."*

ZARINA: (teasing him) *"The pleasure is all mine ... Jinen Sheth ... you must be a Hindu..."*

JINEN: *"A Jain ... Those of us who believe in Ahimsa ... non violence, forgiveness, open and accepting to other people's point of views.."*

ZARINA: *"Yes, I read that Jain philosophy and cosmology is the oldest in the world ... long before Hinduism and Buddhism. I was told that Gandhiji's personal secretary was a Jain monk who taught him about Ahimsa ... Not many people know that Gandhi was not a Jain..."*

JINEN: *"Ahh yes, his father was a Gujarati Hindu ... but his mother was a Jain..."*

ZARINA: *"Yes ... I read Gandhiji's autobiography ... it had a great impression on me as a young woman at Smith College.."*

JINEN: (serious at moments and then teasing...)*"Life is really so simple."* (Pause) (He sips his coffee and munches a donut) *"Can you imagine, tonight is a once in a lifetime "chance" meeting you? Just think, it was miraculous. We both came out of it safe ... I am glad I was driving my motorbike today ... my car is at the shop being repaired. I would have never been so frighten and able to fight those three drunks ... What an adventure. As a Jain, I refuse to cause any harm to anyone ... But I guess we have to protect ourselves.* (Pause) *Since the streets are getting rough with senseless attacks and shootings. Recently, I took classes with my office friends in karate and I received my black belt ... We thought we need to find a way of protecting* *ourselves when we have to work late nights and weekends ... And like you, I am also very ambitious and want to start my own company in the next few years."*

ZARINA: *"It was the will of God, that you came on the motorbike ... It is now me sitting here with you ... I can imagine what may had happened...* (Pause ... teasing) *Unless you think, you could have fought those three drunks with your karate skills like James Bond!"*

JINEN: (Laughing and joking to make the scene lighter...)*"And saved a beautiful damsel in distress ... Reminds you of those romantic novels we read in high school..."*

ZARINA: (Joking back at him)*"Yes ... Like the cartoons we use to watch on TV when we were kids - the only things missing are dragons, those guns and space ships..."*

JINEN: (He notices that Zarina is completely soaked and her hair is wet...)*"Do you think you would like to change your clothes and dry your hair, before I take you home?"*

ZARINA: *"Although I live on my own, I spend three days a week with my parents, especially on weekends and drive home to upstate New York. I have rented a studio apartment in town because; sometimes we have to work late into the night. I am ambitious in becoming a partner in the next five years, I thought a place of my own in the city would give me some time to myself, spend time with my friends and colleagues. I could have taken a cab to my apartment. Or ... may be, you can drop me off, so I can get out of these wet clothes and call my father ... I feel so stupid telling him about what happened tonight..."*

JINEN: *"Well, don't tell him anything ... Let's keep the incident a secret between us ... no one needs to know. Do you have brothers?"*

ZARINA: *"No, I don't have any brothers or..."*

JINEN: *"Boyfriend... husband?"*

ZARINA: "*I have plenty of cousins ... but no boyfriend ... no husband ... as of yet..."*

JINEN: *"Sorry for intruding into your life ... But I feel glad we met...Even though nothing happened, I am sure you must be feeling so vulnerable and scared by the shocking incident! It will really worry your father ... I am sure he is like my own parents. They are so protective ...always worrying so much about us ... they can't understand our need to be independent and the desire for personal privacy ... especially after we work so hard every day. They just do not understand why we need to live on our own ... alone in the city ...* (Pause). *Oh, would you like to dry up at my place, it is only two blocks from here..."*

ZARINA: *"No ... No ... I will take a rain check ... Please drive me to my studio apartment which is about 15 blocks from here.."*

JINEN: (Teasing her)*"Okay, whatever makes you comfortable. Your wish is my command. And tomorrow, I will drive you back, so you can report the incident to the police and they will help us to pick up your car. So we don't worry your father."*

ZARINA: *"Thanks; I really appreciate everything you have done for me ... how can I ever repay you for saving me...?"*

JINEN: *"Lady, I am no Superman or Batman, but merely your knight in shining Armor ... with my motorbike as my black stallion. Maybe, we can have dinner one day?"*

ZARINA:"*OK. I would like that."*

Laughing, they walk together out of Dunkin Donuts and ride off on the Harley Davison motorscooter as though they had known each other for a long time. Like old friends, Zarina is seen jumping on and then jumping off the motorscooter, thanking Jinen for saving her life and walking up the stairs of her brownstone building.

JINEN: *"Good night sweet maid ... don't forget to..."*

ZARINA: *"Lock my door..."*

JINEN: *"And put the keys in a safe place ...My business card and cell phone number ... Remember I am only a phone call away..."*

ZARINA: (Teasing him...) "*That's a comforting thought...*"

SCENES

They meet at the Loew's cinema hall to see the classical Indian movie called Mughal E Azam. Large poster, huge cinema mall.

They walk into Barnes and Nobles. She buys a cookbook and he buys a computer book. They pay separately at the counter, Jinen takes the bag from her hand, and their hands touch.

Scene at a disco dancing place on Park Avenue as they move on the dance floor, they hold hands, and then they dance. As the music goes soft and romantic. Zarina places her arm on his shoulder, they are laughing, and suddenly they are dancing close together.

Song about having met each other in another life ... another place ... another time ...

Both sing.

Hundred times we will reborn for our love
Thousand times we will reborn for our pleasure
Well, Million times we will born for our love
O.K., Darling, Sweetheart
Hey, we both will reborn, reborn, and reborn
Well, Our love cycle will never stop
We both will drive, fly, enjoy, in love all over the world
Hey darling, no nirvana?
Well sweetheart, our love will never be ending
O.K are you sure? Then love is our heaven
Yea, Yea, Yea
Oh dear God, listen to our wishes
Fill up our hearts with Joy, No ending our love ever

Part 2

SCENES

Scene: Camera moves into the surroundings of Jain temple (Siddhi Challum) in New Jersey show blissful scene in the winter snow across the lake and the trees leaves with snow drops dripping, it is early winter and then Spring flowers to show the passage of time, 10-15 years later.

Inside the Ashram, before the statues of Mahavirji and major Tirthankars, there is a man in priest clothes. Close-up of lips moving, reciting prayers, Close-up of eyes closed. Closes up of a shaven head not one hair on his baldhead. He is not of this world, as though he's living in another world. Seated in the back of the temple is a figure of a devotee, eyes closed and praying, as he is part of the walls. Camera will move several times as we wonder at this figure always groping in a distance from the Jain Priest, but always present in the temple. It is important at this stage to create a sense of suspense. Who is this stranger? Why is he always in a distance whenever we see the Jain Priest?

Camera moves on the Young couple who enters the temple, the young man touches the temple bell resounding loudly throughout the place. The Jain priest turns (there must be no familiar recognition of who he is, who he might be, but a plain ordinary Guruji...

With some makeup, there is no recognition that GURUJI IS JINEN. Makeup will show that he appears completely different. Baldheaded (Jain monk custom for hair being plucked from his head) with a white cloth wrapped around his body. Face of a typical priest, except for the eyes ...

Camera concentrates on the face of Deepak, 25 years old man with his fingers barely touching the young blond/red haired woman. Nicole standing next to him in complete reverence of being inside a holy place. She is around 21 years old, her eyes glued on Mahavirji's statue. She watches Deepak's moves in silence. He approaches the temple bell and rings it, then walks towards the priest and bows reaching down to touch his feet. Nicole then moves and shares his gestures.

GURUJI/JINEN: (Holds out his hand and lifts Deepak up...) *"No ... No ... please do not touch my feet, I am not worthy..."*

DEEPAK: *"Guruji ... we need your help and guidance..."*

GURUJI/JINEN: *"Help? Guidance...?"*

DEEPAK: *"We want to get married..."*

GURUJI/JINEN: (He is seen staring into Deepak's eyes ... and then turning to look at Nicole) *"Married? I do not perform marriage ceremonies ... That will be Hindu Guruji..."*

DEEPAK: (Nods his head as though ashamed. Nicole has a helpless, pleading look) *"We need your help!"*

GURUJI/JINEN: *"Mine? What about your parents?"*

DEEPAK: *"No ... No ... Guruji ... Only you can help us ... our parents do not understand what is happening ... They refuse to listen ... they have closed their eyes, ears and their voice is only aggressive insults and anger at our wanting to marry and be together for the rest of our lives..."*

NICOLE: (echoes in a whisper, her hand touches Deepaks and enfolds tightly together) *"Yes, Guruji ... please we need you to make them understand..."*

GURUJI/JINEN: (Sees the desperateness in the eyes of the two people) *"What is your name?"*

DEEPAK: *"Guruji, I am the son of Lalbhai Mehta ... my mother is Trishla Mehta. I am Deepak Mehta. And this is Nicole..."*

NICOLE: (Standing close to Deepak, staring at the priest...)*"Hi, yes I am Nicole Kennedy ...Gurujee..."*

DEEPAK: *"Guruji, We love each other very much and want to get married..."*

GURUJI/JINEN: (Surprised by the words ... His eyes stare ... looking seriously at the young couple standing in front of him) *"Love ... marriage ... a thing of the past...'*

DEEPAK & NICOLE: (Talking in whispers...)*'We love each other and want to get married, but..."*

GURUJI/JINEN:*"I presume that you are both over 21?"*

DEEPAK & NICOLE: (Shake their heads very affirmatively ... looking at each other)

DEEPAK: *'Yes ... but Guruji ... my parents refuse to listen to us ... they won't hear us.... It is as we are speaking ... voiceless in a dark hollow space..."*

GURUJI/JINEN: (Echoes them...)*"Voiceless in a dark hollow space? ... Speaking voiceless...?"*

DEEPAK: *"For weeks now, we have tried to tell them ... I have tried ... but they will not even consider meeting Nicole..."*

NICOLE:*"I can't understand why ...* (Pause) *Deepak told me that his parents refused to meet me ... least of all, now, they will not even listen to his voice ... Do you think they will ever condone our marriage? I respect the fact that we do not wear any leather items - as I am against the cruelty of animals..."*

DEEPAK: *"They told me they had already chosen a wife from a very wealthy family in Mumbai. How can they do that without talking with me ... getting my consent? I had never seen or met the girl they want me to marry. My mother showed me a photograph of a complete stranger. Of course, I began laughing at the suggestion..."*

NICOLE: *"We feel sure we will be happy together ... I love him..."*

DEEPAK: (Stands proudly by her side ... smiling ... aware that Nicole is very confused by the thought of arranged marriages, etc) *"It is so difficult to explain to Nicole that parents feel an obligated - duty bound - to have their children married in the Old Country ... It is a matter of our social and cultural tradition ... ancient traditions. Children accepted their parents choosing a bride or bridegroom for them and their siblings ... Most parents accepted this custom. So what is so* *different now? They simply refuse to understand or accept our feelings are real and genuine ... As they feel that astrologers predicting matching horoscopes and palm readers ... are the only people to decide that the marriage is made in Heaven...?"*

NICOLE: (Smiling at Deepak...)*"Is there some way we can explain to them? That the world has changed ... the world is changing every day ... that living in America is so different. Here, we are brought up so differently ... From childhood through maturity ... we are taught to be opinionated ... independent ... meeting boys and young men so we understand the meaning of human nature ... We choose our school and college friends. We date ... attend parties ... So why can't we choose our life partner? ..."*

DEEPAK:*"I don't understand. My parents invited our next door neighbors' daughter Caroline Jones for my first official date, where I dressed in my first tuxedo suit and escorted her to the graduation dance ... My mother was very friendly with Caroline's mother. After some time, my father even went into export/import business with Mr. Jones ... and we lived next door to each other in Long Island for over ten years..."*

NICOLE: "*Will Deepak be forced to marry the girl chosen by his parents?"*

DEEPAK: "*I never expected my parents to react in this way ... What has changed? Why has their thinking become so outraged? Strange? They have lived in America for over 30 years. I never dreamed they were so old fashioned ... I was never told seriously that I would have an arranged marriage ... Except two months ago. It was when I decided to bring Nicole to meet them. But they refused. They looked shocked. They will not even think of the idea for me to marry her because, they have their mind made* *up. They won't consider seeing her presence in the family home ... I felt sure once they met and talked with her, they would see what a wonderful, kind loving person she is ... We both have so much in common ... our jobs, our personal ambitions, sharing desires of what it means to live the American way of life ... with two ... may be, three children..."*

GURUJI: *"What about your parents, Nicole?"*

NICOLE: *"My mother died of cancer and my father is an alcoholic. He does not care."*

GURUJI: (to Nicole…) *"I am sorry to hear that."*

GURUJI/JINEN: (asking to Deepak...)*"Is Nicole pregnant?'*

DEEPAK: (Whispers) *"No ... Guruji"*

NICOLE: (Her voice trembles as she is unable to understand the parents)*"All this is so unbelievable ... I have done nothing ... except love Deepak ... He is such a wonderful man and we share this awesome humor ... which is great after long hours and busy days in the law firm where I work. I can't understand why they refuse to meet me! It makes no sense ...No matter to them our chemistry match."*

JAIN MONK: (Watching the young couple in bewilderment ... unable to speak)*"Let us sit down and see what can be done..."*

DEEPAK: *"Please talk to my parents ... they attend this Ashram regularly for worship"*.

GURUJI/JINEN: *"They are devoted followers of Mahavirji's teachings."*

NICOLE: *"Yes ...yes ... you are correct ... I read the book on "Mahavirji" that Deepak gave me as a present on my birthday ... For me, the Jain religion is a way of life, Ahimsa, tolerance, It is needed in today's world of violence and terrorism..."*

DEEPAK: *"Although my parents brought me up as a strict vegetarian, and I attend the Jain temple frequently while studying the teachings of Jain Dharma, during my youth and childhood I am not a religious person ... I was born a Jain, but I am not a religious fanatic..."*

GURUJI/JINEN: (In a commanding voice...)*"I hope you know that. The purpose of Jain Dharma is to achieve moksha and seek the liberation of the soul from the bondage of karmas."*

DEEPAK: *"Guruji, you are my ... our only hope ... we have to make my parents understand the realities of life ... You are...'*

NICOLE: *"Our last hope..."*

GURUJI/JINEN: *"You both are placing too much hope and trust in me ... binding me in a whirlpool of..."*

DEEPAK: *"... Hope ... We have no one else who will give us a voice...'*

NICOLE: *"Please ... we desperately need you to understand our feelings of love..."*

GURUJI/JINEN: *"Deepak, I know your mother and father well ... and I will try and see what I can do about this problem..."*

NICOLE: *"Please ... they need to understand how we feel about each other..."*

GURUJI/JINEN: *"I can only try ... But suppose ... Just suppose Deepak ... your parents don't listen ... What would be your next solution?"*

DEEPAK: *"You tell me ... we came here to seek the answer..."*

NICOLE: *"Solution to our problem..."*

DEEPAK & NICOLE: (Whispering together)*"We are sure we will be happy together and want to get married..."*

GURUJI/JINEN: *"Without Deepak's parents' approval? It will break their hearts..."*

NICOLE: *"What about breaking our own hearts and living our lives in misery without each other? ... We have searched for answers to our emotional state of mind.."*

DEEPAK & NICOLE: (Voice together)*"We are both adults ... We know what we are doing. And where our love will take us ... together"*

GURUJI/JINEN: *"Never forget ... in the eyes of your parents ... you will always remain their children ... They fear for the future ... They are full of fear of letting go of the life they created and nurtured into maturity ... You are their pride and joy ... the person they now live to see grow successfully ... For most* *parents ... Or for any closely knit loving family ... LETTING GO of a loved one ... is the most difficult part of separation ... They are loosing you to a stranger ... whom you have chosen to live the rest of your life, without their consent ... There is the fear of being forsaken ... forgotten ... rejected ...*"

DEEPAK & NICOLE: *"None of the above ... We share no such ill-feeling..."*

GURUJI/JINEN (Stares directly at Deepak and Nicole, smiling as)*"Then, what would you both say is the only option ... the only alternative?"*

DEEPAK & NICOLE (Joking...)*"To elope..."*

DEEPAK takes Nicole's hand and together they quietly leave from the side entrance, disappearing into the sunlight. Next moment, Deepak's parents enter the Ashram. Lalbhai Mehta is a man of 60, well fed, dressed in Indian fashion while his wife, Trishla, 50 is well dressed in a silver gray dress (matches the Mercedes Benz) slightly plum, she is a strict vegetarian, neither eating garlic or onions. A woman prone to diets and fasting.

SCENE

LALBHAI MEHTA: (His hand swings the temple bell ... ringing loudly ... announcing his presence before Mahavirji and major Tirthankar statues at the altar)*"Jai Jinendra Swamiji ... what a lovely sunshine afternoon it is ... My wife, Trishla wanted me to take darshan and pray ... We need to pray to God Mahavirji for guidance..."*

GURUJI/JINEN: (Rosery in his hand, Mumpati uncovered)*"Jai Jindera Lalbhai Mehta and Trishlaben ...Welcome ... welcome ...it is always a pleasure to see you both."*

TRISHLA: (Patiently waiting for her husband to stop talking as most beautiful Indian wives are trained to accept...) *"Jai Jinendra Swamiji ... Today I come as a troubled soul ... seeking answers. For our bad karmas in another life..."*

GURUJI/JINEN: *"Troubled soul ... bad karmas in another life...?"*

LALBHAI MEHTA: *"Yes ... bad karmas..."*

GURUJI/JINEN: *"Problems at work?"*

LALBHAI MEHTA: *"No. No ... that I solve in a twinkle of the eye ... This problems must be solved... Immediately ... Deepak, our son wants to get married..."*

TRISHLA MEHTA: *"We are here to offer prayers and flowers to forbid our Deepak's fate..."*

GURUJI/JINEN: *"Forbid his fate? You mean, may you both along the path of Deepak's marital journey..."*

LALBHAI MEHTA: *"Marital journeys ... what are you talking about? Getting Deepak married is not the problem.*

We have already been arranging the wedding for some months..."

TRISHLA MEHTA: *"Especially as Deepak is now successfully settled in his job..."*

LALBHAI MEHTA: *"Yes, I am so proud of my son Deepak ... He refused to work in my diamond business after he graduated from Harvard. Instead he was hired by this multinational 500 American corporation and has become a great success within five years ... I feel nothing but great pride in him..."*

TRISHLA MEHTA: *"He has been our pride and joy since the day I gave birth and held him in my arms..."*

LALBHAI MEHTA: *(Repeats his wife's words, lighting candles (diya)...)"My pride and joy ... my son wants to get married ...We have been searching and finding beautiful girls in India from highly respectful, wealthy families ... from the time he graduated from Harvard ... He insisted before taking responsibility of a wife and family, he wanted to work and provide a good home for his bride, future children and our grandchildren.*

LALBHAI MEHTA: *"Arranging a marriage is no problem. Trishla has already selected two to three beautiful girls in Mumbai..."*

GURUJI/JINEN: *"Problem?"*

TRISHLA: *"Deepak has chosen his own girl..."*

LALBHAI MEHTA:"... *And she is not JAIN! Big Major Problem***..."**

GURUJI/JINEN: *"Oh, Big major problems for you both...?"*

TRISHLA: *"I hope you will understand our problem".*

LALBHAI MEHTA: (Anger in his voice ... as he tries to pray) *"He is Not Marrying a Jain ... He is marrying Nicole..."*

GURUJI: *"So what do you want me to do?"*

TRISHLA: *"Please Gurji ... you must convince Deepak that he cannot marry Nicole ... It has never happened in our family..."*

GURUJI/JINEN: *"Have you both sat down and talked with Deepak? ... Have you both met the girl? ... It is important to meet her and see who she is ... They need you both at this time ... Listen to what they have to say.."*

LALBHAI MEHTA: *"No son of mine is going to marry outside the Jain community ... I have told him ... No son of mine is going to marry Nicole ... He will not listen ... He is stubborn as a mule..."*

GURUJI/JINEN: *"Lalbhaiji ... It seems like your son has his father's determined temperament...*

TRISHLA: *"Guruji, you know ... you have seen ... Religion is very important to us ... Jain Dharma is the faith we taught Deepak ...He couldn't ignore it. I have already chosen the most beautiful girl from the wealthiest Jain family in Mumbai ... She saw Deepak's photograph last month and agreed to marry him. What am I going to tell the family? How can I show my face in Mumbai? This marriage must take place ... I gave them my word of honor."*

LALBHAI MEHTA: *"We know the family since the children started to go to school ... We talked about them getting married to each other ... Padmarati (Indian Girl) is a lawyer in Mumbai, though she attended Princeton University. But she returned home as soon as she graduated. We had Deepak meet her when they were in college ... and during her graduation ... I was so sure that Deepak liked her ... but he did not say a word to me ... He had just graduated ... He told me he was more interested in finding a good job..."*

TRISHLA: *"So we waited ... giving him time ... to settle ... and feel confident and sure of himself ... He's our beloved son ... I cannot ... never ... live without him ... Even now when I don't get to see him on weekends and holidays ... my heart is full of sadness ... I feel so rejected that he prefers the company of his friends over me ...I hate being locked out of his life ... He is our son..."*

GURUJI/JINEN: *"Please ... we need to think carefully ... These days, we must start understanding our children ... most young people show off and talk that way ... but as parents we must start building the generation gap ... when our children complain about mistreatment ... creating misunderstandings by refusing to listen to their parents ... We do not understand that they are no longer children but, young adults ... Did we forget what it was like ... when we were young like them? It seems to have completely disappeared from our memories..."*

TRISHLA: *"Once they go to a university ... they no longer want to return home ... they become so concentrated in their work, their friends ... they want nothing to do with their parents ... ignoring all the love and nurturing we gave them throughout their childhood and youth ... How can they forget?*

I still remember the day Deepak was born ... He was such a beautiful baby..."

LALBHAI MEHTA: *"Listen to yourself. Your Deepak ... is no longer your baby ... Two months ago he announced that he loved this Christian girl and he would like us to meet her ... I was shocked beyond my belief ... My son Deepak tells me he wants to marry this Christian ... I asked him: What is wrong with marrying a Jain girl?"*

TRISHLA: *"We are doing our best to stop him from seeing Nicole ... We have completely rejected meeting her in our home ... We told him we want no part of this kind of wedding ... We have our family honor at stake. He has a duty to listen to us ... and not argue with his father and grandfather ... storming out of the house telling them he did not need their permission to marry the woman he loves..."*

LALBHAI MEHTA: *"Marry the woman he loves ... What does he know about love? My own father, his grandfather, could not believe what he was hearing ... He turned to me and repeatedly asked whether his grandson told us he was marrying his American sweetheart ... My father kept repeating to himself: "this is a family disaster ... our family name will crumble to the dust. There will be no future for my great grand children as Jains ... American woman? Where did he find her?"*

TRISHLA: *"It is impossible to explain to Deepak's grandfather ... I told them they work together in the same office ... She had taken Deepak to meet her parents. I spoke with Deepak's best friend, Arjun who told me in confidence that the Nicole's mother is dying of cancer and her father drinks like a fish ... Deepak does not seem to care about all this ... He told me* *that he loves the girl ... what was her name ... Nicky ... Nilly ...NiColi ...I don't remember?"*

LALBHAI MEHTA: *"He is no longer your son ... If Deepak marries this woman, I will disinherit him completely. I will never speak with him again ... I never want to see him ... How could he do this to us ... his own parents ... to his mother? We would have even accepted a Hindu girl ... but a Roman Catholic woman ... I forbid it.."*

GURUJI/JINEN: *"Now, now ... Patience. Ahimsa ... If you love your son ... you must try and understand ... You both must reason with him ... Please don't close your anger on your child ...We have been living in this country for nearly one hundred years ... Lalbhaiji who have lived as a successful businessman ... We sent our children to the best schools and colleges this country offers. We brought them up as American children; they played baseball and compete in their studies by studying hard. They were so proud of being part of your family as you gave the right principles of living a Jain life ... Now you suddenly decided they are no longer Americans? You have to listen..."*

TRISHLA: *"Oh, No ...He will never disinherit his son ... I will see to that, there is too much love between father and son..."*

LALBHAI MEHTA: *"Are you kidding? If he does not listen to me ... I will certainly disinherit him and cut him off with one penny ...Does a son love by refusing to listen to his father ... disgracing the family traditions?.."*

GURUJI/JINEN: *"No ... just listen to yourselves ... He is your flesh and blood ...What does God Mahavirji say about love and forgiveness? ... He never maintained that whatever he* *said was the only truth. Appana sachmesejja "search the faith within yourself." Nobody can say that the truth searched by Mahavira is obsolete today. God Mahavirji says, "Search the Truth yourself." Think, search and ponder ...Remember Deepak is an adult man."*

TRISHLA: *"Guruji ...I don't understand why you are taking Deepak's side ... We are here to ask your advice... We need to understand what we must do? You must be on our side..."*

GURUJI/JINEN: *"This is not a matter of taking sides ... We need to understand our children ... indirectly, they are begging for love and forgiveness ...They want you to accept them for who they are ... and what they have become as Americans..."*

LALBHAI MEHTA: *"Our children are not Americans. They are from India. No son of mine is going to marry a Christian girl. Deepak has to listen to me ... to his grandfather ... and not break his mother's heart. He must break off this relationship immediately and marry into the Jain family we have chosen ... He cannot question my authority ... I am his father..."*

GURUJI/JINEN: *"Patience ... We must not be so old fashioned and narrow minded ... You know that the bonds of true love are very hard to break, especially among young adults ... especially when they have made up their minds..."*

LALBHAI MEHTA: *"Guruji ... I will deal with my son in our own way ... He has to live the life we have given him ... otherwise he will never enter my home again ... He will be dead in our memory..."*

Angry and outraged at the thought of his son, Lalbhai Mehta and his wife Trishla walk out of the temple door.

Camera follows them as the scene fades away in inaudible conversation echoing in the distance.

SCENE (CHANGES)

Following day Deepak and Nicole enter the Ashram and meet the Guruji who is praying.

DEEPAK: *"Guruji ... Jai Jinendra ... Have you*

had any luck?"

GURUJI/JINEN: *"Deepak, all this has nothing to do with luck ... You have broken your parents heart..."*

NICOLE: *"Guruji, that was not our intention..."*

GURUJI/JINEN:*"I have to confess, I tried to make them understand ... But it was completely hopeless..."*

DEEPAK: *"Like talking to a blank wall ... Voiceless echoes ... except father's voice and mother repeating her own dreams of my arranged marriage..."*

GURUJI/JINEN: *"It is very unfortunate ... they don't seem to understand they are hiding behind religion, ancient traditions that are no longer relevant today ... Yes, I agree with you both, they are taking the easy way out by demanding that Deepak become part of religious rituals ... they do not understand the true meaning of the openness of Jain Dharma ... forgiveness..."*

NICOLE: (Turns to Deepak ... losing faith in the Guruji)*"What will be our next move, dear heart?"*

DEEPAK: *"Don't worry, my love ... we are both adults, not children. We are not backing out on the love we feel for each other..."*

GURUJI/JINEN: *"In the eyes of your parents, Deepak, you will always be their child - their beloved son - I hope and pray that both your decisions will not create unhappiness with a clashing of ill-fated events..."*

DEEPAK: *"Guruji, if you were in my shoes, what would you do...?"*

GURUJI/JINEN: *"Deepak, this is not a fair question to ask a priest ... who has renounced this earthly existence..."*

NICOLE: "*But just suppose...*"

DEEPAK: *"Nicole, we are not being fair to Guruji ... We have no right to ask him this question..."*

NICOLE: Sadly smiling, watching Guruji's face where the camera shocks the audience, for the first time a slight resemblance of Jinen in the face of Guruji. She takes Deepak's hand and together they ask for his blessings, but paying reverence.

GURUJI: *"So what now?"*

DEEPAK: (With Nicole's face next to Deepak)*"We got our answer yesterday ... we plan to elope ... run away and get married..."*

GURUJI/JINEN: *"Patience ... you both are getting the wrong message ... Please be patient ... you both need to think of a better way to compromise ...to avoid the unbearable pain and suffering ... time alone will tell..."*

DEEPAK & NICOLE: *"Please don't worry, Guruji ... We know what we must do ... for our own happiness in the future..."*

The young lovers walk out of the side door and Guruji's hand reaches for the temple bell to awaken the Tirthankars (Jain God statue) to listen to his prayer. That solitary figure at the back of the temple sits still. Who is he? Why is he there? What does he want?

GURUJI/JINEN: (The audience is aware that the Guru is Jinen)*"Oh, Great souls, forgive me for what I have done ... You know the path for them is not to run and hide from the world. I did not mean to offer them my own solution..."*

Camera fades into darkness ...

SCENE (CHANGE)

It is past midnight. There is a frantic phone ringing the echoes resounding in a distance. Someone comes and wakes Jinen (the JAIN GURU) and gives him the cellphone.

JINEN: (Tired and confused in sleep)*"Hello ... hello ... who is there?"*

LALBHAI MEHTA: (Voice on the phone)*"Guruji ... Guruji ... This is Lalbhai Mehta ... Are you there?"*

JINEN: (A look of wonder in his eyes)*"Jai Jinendra ... Yes, yes ... Lalbhaiji I am here ... Please calm yourself ... Is everything all right?"*

LALBHAI MEHTA: (Voice of Trishla is heard shrieking and crying in agony...)*"Jai Jinendra Guruji ... I am trying to calm my wife and myself ... but it seems impossible. It's Deepak..."*

JINEN: *"Deepak? What about Deepak...?"* (Pause) *"What has happened?"*

LALBHAI MEHTA: *"Deepak has run away with that girl..."*

JINEN: *"What? I can't hear you ... run away with Nicole"*

LALBHAI MEHTA: *"He will marry this girl ... He phoned and notified us ... He will not listen to reason ...I informed him that I would be disowning him as my son..."*

JINEN: *"Oh, Blessed Tirthankars' give me the strength to answer a father's plea of agony..."*

LALBHAI MEHTA: *"From today ... Deepak is dead to us ... He is no longer our son ...His mother is weeping constantly. Deepak's grandfather is annoyed. We need to be consoled ... Our lives are over ... our son has gone with his woman ... He has chosen her over our love... over his family honor ... his duty. This is impossible ... How can this happen?"*

JINEN: *"Have faith, Deepak is a good man ... He does not want to break ties with his family. He has no intentions of hurting you all ... Just give him a little time..."*

LALBHAI MEHTA: *"Time?.. What time? ... He has taken his own decision to marry - never considering the family consequences for a moment ... What will we tell our friends ... and the young Jain girl in India who thinks she is going to marry Deepak? Trishla is weeping like a wounded bird whose wings have been broken by Deepak..."*

JINEN: *"We must consider ... think about Deepak ... try and understand the pain and agony Deepak is going through. Consider his point of view...?"*

JINEN: *"Peace ... Forgiveness ... We need to think this matter through with a cool mind ... Remember, Lord Mahavirji and get your strength from him. This too will pass. Keep your faith ... Jai Jinendra"*

The phone conversation ends abruptly by Lalbhai Mehta disconnecting the line. He does not apologize for waking Jinen at an ungodly hour, breaking his sleep. Jinen goes for a walk, as dawn breaks and the first sign of sunlight streak across the sky. After a few hours, he returns to the Ashram and sits in the dinning room for breakfast. There is a television announcing the weather report and then a flash of urgent news of the day.

JINEN: *"Lord Mahavirji ... give us the peaceful wisdom to all understanding and the courage to forgive our loved ones and their actions..."*

Part 3

Few hours later, Jinen unable to sleep, he is sitting in front of the television set in the Ashram library.

JINEN: *"God Mahavirji ... give us the peaceful wisdom to all understanding and the courage to forgive our loved ones for their actions..." (He's Praying)*

Jinen/Jain Priest switches the TV Channel to the local news blaring:

"A police was shot in the chest when he tried to arrest a suspected drug dealer outside the casino.

Police Officer is in critical condition, as the suspect escaped by car...."

"Two masked men robbed a Deli in broad daylight...

Mother arrested after her boyfriend beat her 6-year-old girl ... The child died of fractured head wounds"

JINEN/JAIN PRIEST: *"What is happening in this country? This is moral decay ... senseless killing and ... Is there no good news to be found?"*

TV Anchorwoman on camera appears on television announcing:

"A young couple was found badly injured in a car accident on Highway 745. Police notified family members after identifying the couple as Nicole Kennedy and Deepak Mehta. They are in critical condition, while the driver of the other car was killed instantly..."

JINEN: (Camera on his face ... look of devastating horror as he hears the names of the couple with photographs on the screen)*"Oh, my God Mahavirji ... what have I done? Deepak and Nicole ... they were here a few hours ago ... This is my entire fault. How will I ever forgive myself? ... Oh dear God ... Ahhhhh..."*.

Agonized, Jinen clasps his hand on his chest, as he tries to rise, but falls to the ground. A cry of pain, his face drenched with sweat .The elderly devotee hears his cry and runs into the room. It is Jinen's father who has been the suspicious devotee hovering in the background of the Ashram. Sound of the ambulance echoing as the scene changes from the dawn of darkness into the room of a hospital. Jinen opens his eyes as he finds himself in the hospital bed.

DEVOTEE/FATHER (DHIRAJLAL): *"How do you feel?"*

JINEN: *"Where am I?"*

DEVOTEE: *"In the hospital..."*

JINEN: *"What happened?"*

DEVOTEE: *"The doctor reported that you had a heart attack.."*

JINEN: *"Oh ... I remember ... that sudden pain in my chest..."*

DEVOTEE:" *The doctors almost gave up all hope as I was chanting prayers to God Mahavirji ...but*

JINEN: *"Thank you for your prayer ... in my hour of need."*

DEVOTEE: *"May the peace and blessings of God be with you..."*

JINEN:*"I have noticed you are always at the Ashram praying ... you are everywhere every day ... do you pray for everybody?"*

DEVOTEE: *"Yes ... for forgiveness ... especially for you..."*

JINEN: *"Me? ... But you never said one word to me ... May I ask why you were praying for me?"*

DEVOTEE: (He stands in silence ... looking at Jinen ... unable to speak)

JINEN: *"Forgive me for asking ... why me? Please continue to pray for the entire mankind. I will also join in your prayers."*

DEVOTEE: *"You have every right to ask that question..."*

JINEN: *"We are all devotees living at the Ashram ... complete strangers ... '*

DEVOTEE: *"Correction ... You and I are not strangers ... You are part of my life..."*

JINEN: (Confusion in his face...)*"I have never met you before ... I do not understand...'*

DEVOTEE: *"It is time I explained..."*

JINEN: *"Explained what?"*

DEVOTEE: *"Listen, my son, what I am trying to say ... may be very difficult for you to understand..."*

JINEN: *"You are now talking in riddles..."*

DEVOTEE: *"If you were to recognize me ... you will solve the riddle..."*

JINEN:*"I have never seen you before in my life ... except your eyes look very familiar..."*

DEVOTEE:*"I have been worshipping in the Ashram for three years..."*

JINEN: *"Yes, I have seen you in the temple often. But before that ... you remain a complete stranger..."*

DEVOTEE: *"Look into my eyes ... the eyes of the windows of a man's soul..."*

JINEN: (Looks into the devotee's eyes and nods his head...)*"Also, I find your voice ... reminds me of.."*

DEVOTEE: *"Who does my voice remind you of?"*

JINEN: (Rests his head on the pillow ... closes his eyes...)*"Your voice reminds me of my father ... but he and my mother died in a car accident three ... four years ago..."*

DEVOTEE: (Moves away and stands near the window)*"You are correct ... your father and mother died in a terrible car crash..."*

JINEN: *"Then who are you? Please tell me ... No more suspense..."*

DEVOTEE: (He nods his head, and stands in front of Jinen's bed, whispering...)*"I agree ... no more secrets..."*

JINEN: (Frowning ... his eyes staring at the man in front of him) *"Please? ... No more suspense, I am very confused..."*

DEVOTEE: (Unable to speak the words ... whispers)*"Jinen, I am your father ... my son"*

JINEN: *"Your son? My father? Impossible ... Three years ago I lit the fire on my parents' funeral pyre."*

DEVOTEE: *"Once again you are correct ... But that is only part of the truth..."*

JINEN: (Lifts his head from the pillow ...trying to find some similarity of the man to his father)*"Now I am thoroughly confused ... My father was burned alive with my mother in the car accident..."*

DEVOTEE: *"Please understand ... I am finding it very difficult to talk to you like this..."*

JINEN: (Seated on his bed, staring at the man)*"You? ... My own father? ... This is unthinkable ... unbelievable..."*

DEVOTEE: *"Nothing is unthinkable ...it is the reality in my situation ... It is the truth. Let me try and explain."*

JINEN: (Starts to stand up ... but feels jerky and sits back on the bed)*"What about my Mom? Where is she?"*

DEVOTEE:*"I was the only unlucky survivor ... I wish your mother could be here, instead of me ...She paid dearly for my sin..."*

JINEN: *"Father what sin is you talking about?... why are you talking in riddles again?"*

DEVOTEE: *"Do you remember your life at home?"*

JINEN: *"How does your son forget? it seems like another life ... those good old days in Philly ... at home with you and Mom ... and Zarina..."(Jinen is talking about the past)*

FLASH BACK

SCENE TRANSFER

The close-up face of Zarina evaporates from the past into the present scene. The two young lovers are seen together in the bedroom of Jinen's apartment. Innocently, they are lying in the bed as Zarina snuggles into his arms.

JINEN: *"You are aware that I am completely in love with you? ... Nothing is going to separate us ... We must talk to our parents..."*

ZARINA: *"My parents suspect that I am seeing someone special ... I can't hide it any longer from my father ... I feel I am in seventh heaven all the time ... What about your parents, have you told them about us?"*

JINEN: (Teasing Zarina...)*"I have been hinting to my mother that I have met this beautiful person who has the most lovely eyes and exquisite smile..."*

ZARINA: *"My father has so much faith in me ... I am sure he will listen to my side of our love story before my parents make any harsh judgments..."*

JINEN: *"Let's talk to them together ... once my parents see you ... they will fall in love with you ... just like me..."*

ZARINA: (Teasing me ... in a flirting manner)*"Tell me again ... Was it love at first sight? ... It was for me..."*

JINEN: (Playing back to her teasing...)*"Was it you who saw me first? ... or me who saw you first? I can't seem to remember ... Ah, yes, it was the moment our eyes met..."*

ZARINA: (Face turning serious)*"Tell me seriously ... Have you mentioned my name to your parents?"*

JINEN: (Nodding his head...)*"No ... not yet ... but I will soon ... at the right moment..."*

ZARINA: *"When do you think is the right moment? When is that right moment that we tell your parents? Then, we can meet my Father and tell them ... my parents..."*

JINEN: *"You are right ... I will talk with my Mom and Father first thing tomorrow morning ... I will announce our love to the whole world..."*

ZARINA: *"Jinen loves Zarina and Zarina loves Jinen"*

JINEN: (Holding Zarina's face in his hands, he kisses her gently and she returns the second kiss with more passion in a tight embrace)*"I love you my Zarina"*

ZARINA: *"My love, my true love..."*

JINEN: *"You know, every morning I wake up and whisper your name and most nights I stare at the moon and confess my love for you ... only you, My one and only precious Zarina"*

ZARINA: *"One question, my love, are you sure you love me as your only love?"*

JINEN: (Rises from the bed with a tone of anger in his voice)*"Why are you questioning our love? What is wrong ... especially in the last two days? ... Are you doubting my love for you?"*

ZARINA: *"I was only kidding ... don't look so annoyed ...sometimes the reality of our situation frightens me ... One wrong move and it could wipe out our dreams of love."*

JINEN: (Annoyed by her mistrust of him)*"Zarina ... you are not making any sense ... Are you feeling okay? Did you have a little too much wine at dinner in the Italian restaurant?"*

(Joking, Muslim girl does not drink wine)

ZARINA: *"That depends? I feel so drunk with our love..."*

JINEN: (Abruptly demands)*"Depends on what?"*

ZARINA: *"Depends how you will react to the news I have to tell you?"*

JINEN: *"Please, my love, stop talking in riddles ... If you have something to say, go ahead and tell me ... You are starting to worry me ... I feel you don't love me enough to understand my love for you ... We must be honest with each other..."*

ZARINA: *"You are right ... But I am afraid of your reaction..."*

JINEN: (Reacting to her words, he tries to calm himself and then takes her hands into his clasping them tight)"Y*ou are hurting my feelings ... don't you trust me? What is troubling you, dear heart? Have I done or said something that you are unable to tell me?..."*

ZARINA: *"No, no ... May be, we have done something wrong..."*

JINEN: (Pleads with her by taking her into his arms)*"Please, you must tell me what it is ... I need to understand what you are ... unable to speak ... I have noticed it for the past two days..."*

ZARINA:*"I can't understand why it is becoming more and more difficult to talk to you about it ... when we love each other so much..."*

JINEN: (He thinks his inquiring mind has found the answer)*"Are you worried because of our different religions? Are you afraid it will come between our love and us?"*

ZARINA: *"Our love is too strong ... and we have shared so much together..."*

JINEN: *"Then, what is it?"*

ZARINA: (Takes Jinen's hand and puts it on her stomach)*"I am..."*

JINEN: (Wondering...) *Yea...*

ZARINA: (Slowly with shyness in her eyes...) *"My love, I think I am pregnant..."*

JINEN: *"What? You think ... or are you?"*

ZARINA: (Ashamed starts to weep)*"I am pregnant ... My pregnancy test was positive."*

JINEN: (Moves slight away from Zarina)*"What have you done?"*

ZARINA: *"Excuse me? ... what have I done?"*

JINEN: (Unable to look at the weeping Zarina)*"No, my love, I mean, what have we done? How did this happen? I thought we were both taking precautions."*

ZARINA: (Her face full of tears...)*"You know how it happened, you were there ... We both are responsible, aren't we?"*

JINEN: (Starts to pace across the room...)*"This is not a good start for our love ... Please stops crying ... It is not your fault..".*

ZARINA: (Aware of their predicament, she continues to cry...)*"This is all my fault..."*

JINEN: (A look of frustration...)*"I never said that ... We need to think ... I need to think..."*

ZARINA:*"I hope you are not thinking what I think ... you are thinking..."*

JINEN: (A look of anger)*"Since when did you become a mind reader? We need to find a solution..."*

ZARINA: *"No, please don't think of the solution ... you are talking about our love..."*

JINEN:*"I am aware of it ... May be ... We can get the opinion of a doctor..."*

ZARINA: *"Please don't think of the only solution by most lovers in this country..."*

JINEN: *"Zarina my love..."*

ZARINA: *"I refuse to take a life born by our love..."*

JINEN: (Places his hand on her mouth ... holding her close)*"It never entered my mind..."*

ZARINA: *"It is the only solution to take the easy way out..."*

JINEN: *"Hush ... there are other solutions ... what are you thinking...."*

ZARINA: *"The only solution ... an abortion..."*

JINEN: (Stunned, staring at Zarina in complete silence)

ZARINA: *"Is it your solution ... for this love?"*

JINEN: (Refuses to reply)

ZARINA: *"You men are all alike..."* (Jinen surprise he stands looking at Zarina in silence, his eyes pleading for her understanding)*"Once you get what you want, love flies out of the window..."*

JINEN: (He takes Zarina in his arms, holding her tightly)*"Relax ... We need to think more clearly ... Our love is too precious to destroy..."*

ZARINA: *"Destroy ... If you want to walk out, I will understand..."*

JINEN: (Pleading with Zarina to calm herself)*"Don't talk rubbish ... We need to see this through ... We must tell our parents ... What will your Father say?"*

ZARINA: *"He will probably kill me ... I am so ashamed ... but I love you so much..."*

JINEN: *"No, they are our parents; they cannot be that cruel ... not in this day and age..."*

ZARINA: (Pulling herself together in Jinen's arms and starts to move away)*"I guess, this is becoming my problem. I need to think how I will manage it. I don't want to drag you into the mud of shame..."*

JINEN: (Stands behind her ... and embraces her in his arms)*"It is sad how little you know about me ... I love you and we must do the right thing..."*

ZARINA:*"I am not blaming you ... you are free..."*

JINEN: *"Free? ... from loving you ... the way I love you ... that will never be ...We can no longer think of being free from our love..."*

ZARINA: (Staring Jinen in the face)*"Then ... what is your solution?"*

JINEN: *"Please do not think of an abortion ... This is our love child ... Our adult responsibility ... conceived by our love for each other..."*

ZARINA: *"I thought you would desert me once I told you..."*

JINEN: *"How can you think so little of my love? ... Do you think I was looking for a lover's fling? Telling you I love for my pleasure ... And now that the storm is here, I would abandon you at your hour of need ... How could I stop loving you in this desperate state of mind? ... I love you, Zarina, how can I prove it to you?"*

ZARINA: *"I know ... I seem to have doubted our love..."*

JINEN: *"You still don't know who I am ... though I am so confident of your nature and who you are ... This is our problem - Not your problem. We will find the best solution..."*

ZARINA: *"Jinen, I knew you would feel this way ... but I was scared ... after seeing what has happened to my friends and I was so frightened that you would blame me..."*

JINEN: *"Blame you, I love you and welcome the news. You made me very happy..."*

ZARINA: *"Jinen my love..."*

JINEN: *"You must have no more doubts ... Say no more ... We have to accept this problem and solve it by accepting our responsibility ... for a healthy and happy child..."*

ZARINA: *"Oh, my loving prince ... I was sure that you were different from other men ... please forgive me for doubting your integrity..."*

JINEN: (He kneels before her ... kissing her hands...)*"I understand ... my love. I guess if I found myself in your situation, I may have doubted the man ... Zarina, my princess of love, Will you marry me?"*

ZARINA: (She kneels before Jinen and embraces him)*"Jinen, my lover ... my only true love ... I will marry you ... but first we must tell our parents..."*

JINEN: (Lifts her up into his arms ... theme song ... music is heard everywhere...)*"Our love has solved the first battle ... now we have to prepare ourselves for war..."*

ZARINA: *"War? I wish I had a magic wand ... One flick ... and all our wishes would come true..."*

JINEN: *"We must face the war tomorrow ... within 24 hours..."*

ZARINA: *"And for the rest of my life ... I am yours and you are mine ... The very thought is so frightening and yet I feel so alive..."*

JINEN:*"I agree it is frightening ... but we are two adults ... and no matter what, we will get married. I promise you, my love..."*

ZARINA: *"I don't need your promise any longer ... I am so sure about you ... and who you really are ... an honorable man..."*

JINEN: (Takes Zarina in his arms)*"My honorable woman, my true love..."*

SCENE dissolves with the haunting theme song playing for the moment.

Part 4

SCENE

Jinen's confesses to his parents about Zarina. Father is seated at the head of the dinning table in Jinen's home, while his mother appears with warm dishes of food and serving her husband and son at the table.

SHARDA/ (JINEN'S MOM): (Pampering her son and husband to eat more...)*"Take one more poori"* (bread)

DHIRAJLAL (JINEN'S DAD): (serves himself rice, while he starts to eat with his hand)*"The doctor told me to watch my calories. He says I am over weight and I must watch my blood pressure..."*

SHARDA: *"Nonsense ... what does these doctors know? ... they don't eat and they don't allow anyone else to eat..."*

DHIRAJLAL: *"Doctors are very well qualified in this country ... they know what they are saying..."*

SHARDA: *"Is it a doctor's business to tell you what to eat and what not to eat? ... They have to take care of our health, not eating habits..."*

DHIRAJLAL: *"You know I have a problem with high blood pressure..."*

SHARDA:*"I am not a rocket scientist, but I know one poori will not harm you..."*

DHIRAJLAL: *"Well, if it makes you happy, then I will take one..."*

SHARDA: *"And what about you Jinen, my precious son..."*

JINEN: (his mouth full of food ... nods his head in silence)

SHARDA: (She serves more food on his plate *"My beloved son, eat more ... you look thin and worried ... And you do not have blood pressure problems..."*

JINEN: *"Mom, No more, please ... I have been eating fast..."*

SHARDA: *"Jinen, my son, since yesterday ... you are here and then you are not here ... what is troubling you?"*

JINEN:*"I am here, Mom ... Nothing is troubling me..."*

SHARDA: *"Is there something you want to tell us?"*

DHIRAJLAL: *"Any problems at work ... with the job?"*

JINEN: *"No, no ... Yes..."*

SHARDA: *"Look at him ... See how he is answering you ... I know something is wrong..."*

DHIRAJLAL: *"Sharda, Jinen is not a kid ... He is an adult ... Why do you worry he is still your little boy?"*

SHARDA: *"He will always be my little boy in my eyes ... I know he is all grown up, but that's what worries me..."*

JINEN: *"Mom, Dad, I am fine ... My work is fine..."*

SHARDA: *"Then, why are your eyes so troubled?..."* (She turns to her husband)*"Did you talk to Jinen about Sureshbhai?"*

DHIRAJLAL: (He nods his head and then clears his throat)*"Oh, yes, Jinen, Your mother reminded me that we have something important to discuss ... You remember Sneha?" (Indian Girl who is a candidate to marry Jinen)*

JINEN: *"You mean Sureshbhai's (Indian girls Father) daughter?"*

DHIRAJLAL: *"Yes, son ... what do you think about her?"*

SHARDA: *"She is such a nice loving girl..."*

JINEN: *"Yea, she is a nice girl..."*

DHIRAJLAL: *"Yes, I introduced you to her at the last wedding we attended when her father Sureshbhai spoke with us..."*

JINEN: *"Yes, we have met at the Ashram and some parties. That's about it."*

SHARDA: *"Would you be interested to know more about her? We can arrange it..."*

JINEN: *"No, no ... not particularly..."*

SHARDA: *"Dear son, her parents approached us..."*

JINEN: *"For what? For donations?"*

SHARDA: *"No, my son, they like you very much ... they admire you ... They noticed how ambitious you are and how hard you work..."*

JINEN: *"That's cool..."*

DHIRAJLAL: (He clears his throat and stares at his son with a touch of annoyance)"*Now, don't act so naive ... They are interested and looking for a boy from a good family for their daughter Sneha"*

JINEN: (Looking exasperated and yet playing it innocent)*"That's good news ... I am so happy for Sneha...'*

DHIRAJLAL: (Anger in his voice)*"You know what your mother and I are saying ... Don't act indifferent. They suggested your name for their daughter"*

JINEN: (Stands up and walks towards the frige to get a bottle of water)*"I am sorry, I am not interested in her..."*

DHIRAJLAL: *"May I ask you why?"*

JINEN: *"You may, father...'*

DHIRAJLAL: *"Thank you. So what is your answer?"*

JINEN: (He drinks a glass of water ... stalling for time)*"I will not marry her..."*

SHARDA: *"But you just said she is a nice girl....'*

JINEN: *"Yes, Mom, she is a nice girl*

SHARDA: *Then, what is wrong with you?"*

JINEN: "*Nothing..."*

SHARDA:*"I think it is time for you to settle down ... marry and have children..."*

JINEN:*"I agree..."*

SHARDA: *"That makes me very happy ... Should we accept Sureshbhai's proposal?"*

JINEN:*"I don't think it will be possible..."*

DHIRAJLAL: *"Do you have somebody else in mind?"*

SHARDA: *"Yes, that lovely girl who phones ... she phoned yesterday and politely asked for you..."*

JINEN: "*Yesterday?"*

SHARDA: *"After the phone call, you rushed out of the house and disappeared. You did not even hear me asking "tell me my son, who is this girl?"*

JINEN: *"I have been meaning to tell you all ... I was going to bring her home to meet you all..."*

DHIRAJLAL: "*Is she some girl friend of yours?"*

JINEN: *"Something like that, Dad. We met some months ago ... and I was planning to bring her home to meet you folks..."*

MANGLABEN (JINEN'S GRANDMOM): *"I hope she is a nice Jain girl..."*

JINEN: (Moving towards his grandmother and puts his arms around her) *"Oh, yes, Grandma, she is a very nice girl.*

Beautiful, you will love her..."

MANGLABEN: (Kissing him on his forehead and then places her hand on her ears, as she is hard of hearing)*"Did you say a nice Jain girl?*

JINEN: *"She is a very nice girl..."*

MANGLABEN: *"Jinen, listen to me..."*

DHIRAJLAL: (Turns to the older woman, his eyes on Jinen's face)*"Mother, please let him finish telling us what he is trying to say...'*

JINEN: *"Thanks Dad, I want to tell you all that I am in love..."*

MANGLABEN: *"Look at this young generation, in love ... what do they know about love and marriage?"*

JINEN: "*Grandma, Dadiji, this is the end of 19th century How can I explain my happiness?"*

DHIRAJLAL: (His lips quivering ... his eyes turning angry with impatience) *"Mother, please do not get upset ... We all trust Jinen, he will never let us down..."*

SHARDA: *"Jinen, where did you meet this girl? Do we know her parents? Is she from here?"*

JINEN: *"Mom, please calm yourself… She was born here and works in as financial manager in the bank. No you have not met her parents, but they live in up State New York."*

DHIRAJLAL: *"That's a relief my son…"*

SHARDA: *"What is her name? Her family name?"*

JINEN: *"Would you like to meet her?*

DHIRAJLAL: *"Yes, yes, son, we all will be glad to meet her. When will you bring her?"*

JINEN: "*… To the house?"*

DHIRAJLAL: *"Of course, unless you prefer that we meet her and her family in a restaurant?"*

JINEN: *"Let's see … I will tell her and we will plan to get together of our two families … as soon as possible…"*

SHARDA: *"You have been hiding her from us … Why did you not bring her home sooner?"*

DHIRAJLAL: *"Sharda, keep your suspicious mind to yourself. You know our son will never do anything wrong … Now, don't go upsetting yourself and my mother. Jinen, knows what he is doing … we have brought him up to be respectful to his elders feelings…"*

SHARDA: (She goes to the older woman and they hug each other) *"Ma, what do you think? ... He has been hiding her away from us..."*

MANGLABEN: (Exasperated, she gets up and walks out of the dinning room fuming) *"What can I say? I never approved of permitting Jinen to live in his own apartment in the city. But nobody listened to me. It was more family expenses ... even though he was earning a good salary ... It would never have been permitted by his grandfather, if he was alive."*

SHARDA:*"I am feeling very uncomfortable with this news..."*

DHIRAJLAL: *"May I ask why...?"*

SHARDA: *"Look at the way he is talking ... the girl is definitely…"*

JINEN: *"Mom, please control yourself ... Yes, you are right. She is not a Jain..."*

SHARDA: (At the verge of screaming ... turning to her husband) *"See what I told you ... I was right ... I knew it from the beginning..."*

JINEN: "*Mom, please don't react this way ... I will not bring her to the house. Just let's forget it..."*

DHIRAJLAL: (He stands up, there is anger in his face)*"Listen, both of you. Calm down. Sharda, Jinen can bring the girl here. This does not mean, we accept his choice, right?"*

JINEN: *"Then, why go through the charade ... pretending to have an open mind ... I cannot have Zarina go through it..."*

DHIRAJLAL: *"Zarina? Who is she? That may be the reason you were meeting her secretly. Your mother and I want to see the girl of your choice. Bring her home. But we will not agree with you to arrange the wedding."*

JINEN: *"Her name is Zarina. Fine, I will bring her tomorrow, but please understand ... our minds are made up, Dad. We are both adults."*

SHARDA: *"Adults ... then why were you ashamed of introducing her to us? ... You don't care about any advice we had given you?"*

JINEN: *"Mom, this is my life ... this is our life..."*

DHIRAJLAL: *"But it affects all of us too ... What you do with your life is our concern ... we brought you up as a responsible citizen... Let's not discuss it any further. You bring her home and we will decide! ..."*

JINEN: (He stares at his parents and walks out of the room)*"We have decided to get married ... I hope you both will give your consent when she comes..."*

SHARDA: (She wants to say something, but her husband places his finger on his lip to warn her to be quiet)*"When who comes ... who is she..."*

SCENE (Shows characterization of Jinen's parents in the dinning room)

SHARDA: (Sits in the chair and turns to her husband)*"How can you allow this to happen?"*

DHIRAJLAL: *"Listen, it looks like we do not have any choice in this matter at the present time. We brought up the subject of marriage. We need to be patient and if you push him too hard, we will loose our son ... forever..."*

SHARDA: "*So, my son Jinen will marry anyone he wants?"*

DHIRAJLAL: "*Sharda, this is the end of the 19th century..."*

SHARDA: *"But, he is our son."*

DHIRAJLAL: *"Yes, Yes, he is our son, but this is America."*

SHARDA: "*Remember, when Jinen was only five years old, I told you let's go back home, but you wanted to stay in America a few more years and now a life time has passed ... And our son is a man..."*

DHIRAJLAL: *"Our son thinks he is an independent American and we have had a very good life here, we have been perfectly happy..."*

SHARDA: *"Until now... this will be the end of our happiness ... if we don't do something about it..."*

DHIRAJLAL: *"Well, the bright side is that Jinen wants to get married ... So many children are refusing their parents..."*

SHARDA: *"For me ... for me ... I see darkness everywhere ... who is this girl? Why did he not tell us?... there is something wrong?"*

DHIRAJLAL: "*You are worrying about nothing...*"

SHARDA: *"The moment he said, I will marry ... my heart sank..."*

DHIRAJLAL: *"Why don't we drink a cup of tea? ... it will relax us ... we need to think carefully how to solve this problem..."*

SCENE changes to Jinen, sitting in his room, talking on his cellphone. He sounds agitated, but tries smiling as he speaks.

JINEN: "*Hey, my love...*"

ZARINA: (Split screen)*"I miss you ... Do you miss me?"*

JINEN: " *A wee bit...*"

ZARINA: *"That's the reason you are phoning me..."*

JINEN: *"No, no ... I have to share something with you..."*

ZARINA: *"Share something ... what?"*

JINEN: *"What?"*

ZARINA: *"Did you tell your parents about us?"*

JINEN: *"Yes, we talked during dinner and I told them everything..."*

ZARINA: "*Everything? ...*"

JINEN: "*No ... not that ... No I did not mention that...*"

ZARINA: *"Oh, I see..."*

JINEN: "*The good news is that they want to meet you ...tomorrow*"

ZARINA: (Teasing him ... but happy)*"And the bad news is..."*

JINEN: "*We are on our own ... we have to convince them that we really and truly love each other ... no matter what...*"

ZARINA: "*Did you say tomorrow? I feel faint...*"

JINEN: "*Hey, my true love, don't faint on me, we need our strength tomorrow...*"

ZARINA: "*Tomorrow? ... I am terrified ... scared at meeting your parents....*"

JINEN: "*I told you, I am with you one hundred percent...*"

ZARINA: "*Yes, Jinen, I know that now ... How could I have ever doubted you?*"

JINEN: "*You should have seen me ... telling both my parents and grandmother that we will be getting married...*"

ZARINA: "*Did you say my name and that I am not a Jain?*"

JINEN: "*Not directly ... but we will come to that bridge when the time comes...*"

ZARINA: "*I feel a storm (toofan) coming, blowing away the bridges leaving us nothing to cross...*"

JINEN: (Teasing her) "*Zarina darling ... Are you having some kind of a bad dream or what?*"

ZARINA: "*Like any woman, I am worried ... Is that wrong?*"

JINEN: "*Leave all the worrying to me ... You just dress up and show them how beautiful you really are...*"

ZARINA: "*Will that be enough for them to accept me?*"

JINEN: "*More than enough ... they will see your beautiful soul and love you as much as I love you ... I will come by and pick you up...*"

ZARINA: "*One moment, my love, How should I dress? Should I wear a saree or salvar? What should I say when I meet them? Are there any customs that I have to follow? Shall I bring a gift? ... May be some flowers? ...*"

JINEN: "*Please no formalities ... Just be your wonderful self. We are not putting on a show. I will handle my parents.*"

ZARINA: "*You make it sound so simple ... Why didn't we meet them before?*"

JINEN: "*Everything is so simple on the surface...*"

ZARINA: "*And you are not worried?*"

JINEN: "*Well, I had my doubts when I blurred and announced we will marry after they meet you...*"

ZARINA: "*Then, I will try and do my part to compliment your hard work...*"

JINEN: "*You my love will be perfect. After all you are only meeting my parents, not some monsters from outer space...*"

ZARINA: "*You mean, my future in-laws?*"

JINEN: "*One thing at a time. You forget we have to deal with your parents too. Then I will see what you have to say to your father...*"

ZARINA: "*Oh, yes ... I had forgotten my parents ... but if we get the approval of your parents then father may not mind ... I know him. Gosh, I will not be able to sleep tonight...*"

JINEN: "*Think about me and you will fall asleep ... That's what I do ... think of you...*"

ZARINA: "*If I stop thinking about you, I think I will die - You have become every breath of my life...*"

JINEN: "*Don't loose that thought ... so we can dream about a long and happy married life together...*"

ZARINA: "*Dreams together don't always come true...*"

JINEN: "*Well, dreams do come true if we are realistic about what we want and need - and we love each other... There is nothing greater than the love of a man for his woman. We will make our destiny together...*"

ZARINA: "*How poetic you can get Jinen? I love your positive attitude to life. That's the one quality of our love that I cherish. See you and your parents tomorrow*"

JINEN: "*That's the spirit, my love...*"

ZARINA: "*But we must be honest with your parents and tell them I am...*"

JINEN: "*I agree ... there is nothing to hide ... We love each other*"

ZARINA: "*Is there anything I need to know ... any questions your parents might ask?*"

JINEN: "*Hey, Please just be you ... no pretense ... just be yourself ... Have no fear in your heart...*"

ZARINA: "*God's willing*"

JINEN: (Flips the cellphone closed and lies on the bed...) "*Goodnight, my true love....*"

Part 5

SCENE - Next day at Jinen's home, his Father, mother and grandmother are seated in the family room as Jinen and Zarina enter.

DHIRAJLAL: (Standing to greet them ... his hands folded together...) *"Come in ... come in."*

ZARINA: (dressed in a saree, looking very beautiful, smiling gracefully, with a touch of anxiety in her eyes)

"Namaste (Hi I respect to meeting you)..." (and turns to Jinen's mother and grandmother) *"Nameste...(Hi I respect to meeting you)"*

There are a few moments of confusion, as the mother and grandmother whisper together and then stare at Zarina. Jinen directs Zarina to a sofa chair, while he sits next to his grandmother, after introducing Zarina to his parents)

ZARINA: (She knows everyone is staring at her so she feels very self-conscious...) *"I am happy to meet you all..."*

DHIRAJLAL: (He is taken aback with Zarina's beauty ... but he is surprised when they realize she is a Muslim...) *"Thank you for visiting us ... We are happy to meet you..."*

(He turns to his wife) *"Sharda, ask our guest what she would like?"*

SHARDA: (She gets up from the sofa and plays the hostess) *"Zarina, would you like to have some tea, coffee or juice? Or may be some wine?"*

JINEN: *"Mom ... You never keep wine at home..."*

ZARINA: *"Please don't worry ... It is not necessary..."*

SHARDA: *"We always treat visitors as our guests..."*

ZARINA: *'I hope you don't consider me as a visitor ... or a guest..."*

JINEN: *"She will be part of our family..."*

SHARDA: (Completely ignoring Jinen's remark) *"You have to take something ... tea? Or orange juice?"*

ZARINA: *"I will have a glass of orange juice please..."*

SHARDA: (She turns to Jinen ... her eyes show she is annoyed and irritated by him) *"Anything for you Jinen?"*

JINEN: *"I will take the same as Zarina ... orange juice. Thank you."*

SHARDA: (Walks towards the kitchen ... she still looks annoyed...)

ZARINA: (She feels the mother's annoyance and get up to help...) *"May I help you?"*

SHARDA: *"No, no, you just sit down. I can manage two glasses of orange juice."*

DHIRAJLAL: *"Jinen, how about introducing Zarina?"*

ZARINA: **"***I come from the Christian family ... my father is David Christian, and my mother is Naseembanu "*

MANGLABEN: (Pretending to be hard of hearing...)*"What did you say? ... I did not hear you ... repeat yourself ... what did you say?"*

ZARINA: (Turns to grandmother and repeats herself) *"My name is Zarina, I am David Christian and Naseembanu's only daughter"*

SHARDA: (Enters the room and realizes that Zarina is a Muslim, as she serves them orange juice glasses) *"Oh, dear, oh dear..."*

JINEN: (He turns to his mother and whispers) *"Mom, you promised..."*

SHARDA: (She ignores Jinen and stares at her husband demanding his comments) *"Are you listening, She is David Christian's and Naseembanu's only daughter?"*

DHIRAJLAL: (Taken up by Zarina's beauty and composure) *"Zarina ...David Christian's only daughter..."*

MANGLABEN: (Takes her prayer beads and chants the name of Mahavirji over and over again) *"Jinen, what kind of joke is this? Have you no shame treating your parents and me with this shock?"*

JINEN: "*Grandma, This is no joke. We love each other...*"

SHARDA: *"What about us? ... Don't you love us any more?"*

JINEN: "*Mom, please be reasonable ... You know I love you, father and Grandmother...*"

ZARINA: (Places the orange juice glass on the side table and stands up) *"May be, I should leave ... I am very sorry. I am not here to cause a family feud ... or any ill feelings..."*

JINEN: (Walks up to Zarina and stops her) *"No, Zarina, please don't leave. Your leaving will not change this situation ... This is our future we are talking about"*

(He turns to his parents) *"Mom, Dad, Zarina and I love each other, but I also love you both. There is no doubt in this reality."*

MANGLABEN: (Stands up to leave the room ... she moves slowly...) *"Jinen, my grandson, we are Jain. Why are you complicating your and our lives?"*

JINEN: *"I am not trying to complicate our lives ... You both have always told me that our religion does not discriminate ... that we accept all religious beliefs. We live in America where Interfaith has become such a issue ... and acceptance and forgiveness is the most important in life."*

MANGLABEN: (Reaches the end of the room and stands at the doorway) *"Jinen, there are certain boundaries we never consider to cross..."*

JINEN:*"I will not accept human-made ... artificial ... boundaries. We are good human beings and love each other..."*

DHIRAJLAL: (Watching Zarina and Jinen in silence...) *"Let's not make this meeting any worse than it really is ... We are all civilized"* (He turns and looks at Zarina) *"Have you talked with your parents about Jinen?"*

ZARINA: **"***No. Not yet. We felt ... Jinen felt he must tell you all first - you are the first to know..."*

SHARDA: **"***All this no longer matters"* (She turns to her husband) *"Let's stop everything now and here."*

DHIRAJLAL: (He nods his head ... and watches the two young lovers) *"Please Sharda, let's not rush this ... We need to know what is really happening..."*

SHARDA: **"***I refuse to think this ... situation ... will work ... There is no future to it ... None whatsoever. Please inform Jinen that we do not approve. Make him stop all this nonsense, before our family honor and our own feelings are destroyed..."*

JINEN: **"***Mother, please try and understand..."*

SHARDA: **"***There is nothing to understand. You simply do not care about your father, your grandmother and my feelings..."*

JINEN: **"***That's not true. Otherwise, I would have married her ... We do not need your permission. We are both adults."*

SHARDA: **"***If you both are adults, you can see what is happening ... You cannot marry her. Stop right now."*

JINEN: "*It is not possible...*"

DHIRAJLAL: *"Jinen, it looks like you both have already made up your minds."*

JINEN: "*Yes, Dad ... but I thought you would understand...*"

DHIRAJLAL: "*I am trying ... but you are making things very difficult ...for all of us ... You are no longer seeking permission...*"

JINEN: "*Permission to marry ... No, I needed your blessings ... I will marry Zarina, we have to...*"

ZARINA: "*Jinen, I told you yesterday, you don't have to...*"

JINEN: "*Zarina, I need you to support me ... You know that we love each other, no matter what our parents have to say. So be my strength.*"

DHIRAJLAL: "*Jinen, why are you behaving so stubborn? Listen to Zarina. She understands what all this means more than you do. What is compelling you that you must marry her over our objections?*"

JINEN: "*Father, I told you I love her...*"

DHIRAJLAL: "*Yes, we understand you love her ... and*"

JINEN: "*And you should also know, that I am going to be a father...*"

MANGLABEN: (Standing at the door cries out aloud)

"Satyanash (everything is going wrong)...'

DHIRAJLAL: "*What? What are you saying?"*

SHARDA: (She almost faints at Jinen's words) "*Oy Ma ... Oh, God Mahavir prabhuji ... forgive my son for his sin ... What will people say?"*

DHIRAJLAL: (Rushes to his wife who is on the sofa ... gulping for air ... shaking frantically...) "*Sharda, are you all right? ...Sharda, compose yourself. Jinen are you trying to hurt your mother? Sharda, are you okay?"*

SHARDA: (opens her eyes) "*I would rather die than ... hear what our friends and neighbors will say ... this gossip will ruin our lives ... our family reputation..."*

JINEN: (Almost shaking with determination ...unable to understand why his parents are responding in this shameful manner) "*What about MY life? ... MY future? ..."*

DHIRAJLAL: "*Please Jinen, please keep your voice down..."*

JINEN: "*I thought this was my home ... my parents who would understand and accept Zarina into our home..."*

SHARDA: "*What will we tell our family and friends? We will be the laughing stock ... I am so ashamed. Why did we come to America? For this terrible news... For this... our only son rejecting us..."*

JINEN: "*Mom, stop behaving like an Indian. This is America!"*

DHIRAJLAL: "*Don't talk to your mother in that tone. You may live in America, and you may think it gives you absolute freedom to say or do anything... But you are our son... we brought you with in the Jain tradition and expect you to be more considerate...*"

JINEN: "*I was being considerate in showing you what and how I felt... and hoping for your understanding...*"

SHARDA: "*You should be begging your father for forgiveness for what you have done...*"

JINEN: "*No... I have done nothing wrong... You both always taught me to do what I think is right without any fear or pressure...*"

SHARDA: "*Somehow, my son, I am sure this girl, this Zarina... has coached you on what you are saying ... You are not my Jinen talking ...* "

JINEN: "*Mother, wise up... this is your Jinen... you son... talking*"

ZARINA: *"Please... I have told Jinen he must not feel responsible for our love...'*

DHIRAJLAL: (Turning to the two young lovers) "*So you both are happy with all this grief you are causing now?*"

JINEN: "*Father, honestly, this should not have happened. I don't intend to back out now. It will be immoral. We did not come to this decision over night. We have been seeing each other for some time now. The decision to marry was mine and mine alone. It has nothing to do with Zarina being pregnant. She is* *my love and my life. I plead to you, mother and grandmother to accept her as my wife."*

SHARDA: "*I refuse to throw my religion out of the window. I will not and never agree to this marriage. I must have done some bad deeds and sinned in the past, to have to face this tragic karma today..."*

MANGLABEN: "*Jinen, my grandson. No, you are no more my grandson... You have said enough. Enough is enough! Listen to your parents and stop all this argument. You are still their child... my son's son..."*

JINEN: "*Grandma, I respect your feelings ... I am 25 years old. I am no longer a child. I have been taught by them to make my own decisions and take responsibility of what I decide."*

MANGLABEN: "*So whatever you have been taught you want to give up for her? ... Respect for your elders ... most of all ... your parents ... you refuse to listen any longer?"*

JINEN: (Turns to his father and looks him straight in the eyes) "*Dad, you all are not even giving us a chance. Zarina is a wonderful girl and will make us all very happy..."*

ZARINA: "*Yes Daddymaa (Grandma) ... please forgive us ... and give me a chance to prove myself and how much I love your son..."*

MANGLABEN: "*This marriage will not happen. No matter what you both have done. There is no future in this marriage. Girl stay within your own community... there are too many limits to overcome..."*

JINEN: "*Grandma, this woman is my future wife ... there is no question about our marriage...'*

DHIRAJLAL: (Loudly shouts out to Jinen) "*Jinen, watch your mouth, when you speak to your grandmother. I will not tolerate your behavior in my house!*"

JINEN: "*Dad, respect has to come from both sides. I thought at least you would understand ... man to man...*"

DHIRAJLAL: "*I am sorry son. I have to take your mother's and grandmother's side. We belong to our community and did not consider becoming one hundred percent American. We taught you all the traditions ... all those religious and cultural differences while you were growing up ... towards a purer richer life...*"

JINEN: "*Father, it is not a matter of taking sides. This is my life ... My life with Zarina - the woman I love. I will not permit anyone to come between us ... not you nor my family nor hers. We will marry without your blessings...*"

ZARINA: (She takes Jinen's hands and they start walking out of the entrance door) "*Jinen, please consider what you are saying ... you are their only child...*"

DHIRAJLAL: "*Jinen, Wait.*" (The young couple turns around). "*I think you are making a terrible mistake. Don't burn the bridge between you and your family...*"

JINEN: "*I thought we were trying to build a bridge of understanding between us...*"

DHIRAJLAL: "*If you walk out of that door, then everything will be over. You will no longer be our son. You will loose us forever.*"

JINEN: "*Dad, I know what I must do. I am your son. I will always be your son. But I cannot turn away from my responsibility my love and my child. You have taught me good values. There is nothing that will permit me to throw away those values. You all know that you are being unfair.*"

The two young lovers walk into the night as the song plays into the night leaving behind a mother weeping desperately in the arms of her husband.

Song.

Love is blind, Hey, Hey,
They are never going to stop now.
Love comes from the heart.
Love breaths from right.
They both will spread their blood
Cherish their dreams.
Please understand,
Let them have a new life.
Pray for their bright, successful
Prosperous, love full future.
Please god let them go,
Let them go,
Let them go,
Let them go.

PART 6

SCENES ...

After Zarina's death, a few days later. Jinen is seen unshaven, bloody eyed, and hair ruffled. Scene of frustration as he shows signs of trying to commit suicide, But it is his American friend Kevin Cohen (who is a young Buddhist American) who is seen driving him to the ER in the middle of the night.

Scene opens in the hospital with Dr. Rajiv Gandhi and Kevin in discussion.

DR. RAJIV GANDHI: (His hand on Kevin's shoulder as they walk in the corridor...) "*Kevin, I am so glad you brought Jinen here ... What happened?*"

KEVIN: "*I am not sure ... It is not like Jinen ... I think he took an overdose of pills...*"

DR. GANDHI: "*Sleeping pills ... He smells like he has also been drinking...*"

KEVIN: "*I don't know...*"

DR. GANDHI: "*You reached him in time ... the last few minutes, his condition was touch and go...*"

KEVIN: "*Yea, he's been in bad shape since the death of Zarina ... so depressed. I'm glad I had gone to see him last night. All he did was talk about her ...repeating her name ... over and over again ... Blaming himself for her death. Feeling so helpless ... unable to cope with anything...*"

DR. GANDHI: "*You should have phoned somebody for help ... some family member...*"

KEVIN: "*I wanted to call his parents, but he forbid me ... So I decided to stay with him...*"

DR. GANDHI: "*Life has not been kind to him*"

KEVIN: "*I was lying on the sofa ... when I heard a loud thud! Sound from his bedroom ... I rushed to find Jinen on the floor, with a empty bottle ... I tried shaking to wake him, but he was completely unconscious ... with no sign of life ... So immediately I phoned 911 for the ambulance and then phoned you...*"

DR. GANDHI: "*You did the right thing ... He owes his life to you...*"

KEVIN: "*We need to call his Dad...*"

DR. GANDHI: "*You need to get some sleep ... I will phone his father...*"

KEVIN: "*No, I want to wait and see how he is doing before I leave....*"

DR. GANDHI: "*Kevin, you saved his life ... he is lucky to have a friend like you ... Just relax on the chair, I will let him know...*"

Scene changes to the morning in the Hospital's ICU

DR. GANDHI: (Examining Jinen on the bed...) *"Jinen, how are you feeling...?"*

JINEN: "*Numb ... where am I?"*

DR. GANDHI: "*You tried to overdose on sleeping pills..."*

JINEN: "*Yea ... Gosh, my headaches ... I feel so terribly depressed..."*

DR. GANDHI: "*I can understand what you are going through ... with your personal agony of your parents disowning you as their son and the loss of Zarina..."*

JINEN: "*How am I alive, with everyone I loved is gone? ... My life is not worth living any more..."*

DR. GANDHI: "*You are young ... you have your whole life ahead of you..."*

JINEN: "*No, Dr. Gandhi, I do not wish to live any longer..."*

DR. GANDHI: "*Don't talk this way ... think ... clear your mind..."*

JINEN: "*For the past few days, I tried ... to understand ... question what happened ... Why Zarina? Why not me?"*

DR. GANDHI: "*I could not believe my ears, I agree, it was a heinous crime..."*

JINEN: "*It's unbelievable ... All I can think about is revenge: killing whoever did this crime...*"

DR. GANDHI: "*Jinen, Calm yourself. You already tried to take your own life...*"

JINEN: "*Why did you save me? ... life is not worth living without Zarina...*"

DR. GANDHI: "*It is my job to save lives....*"

JINEN: "*I have no desire to live...*"

DR. GANDHI: "*It will not bring Zarina back to life...*"

JINEN: "*What is life without her? ... all I feel is that I want to join her...*"

DR. GANDHI: "*Do you really think Zarina wants you to join her?*"

JINEN: (Silently whispered...) "*We loved each other ... more than life...*"

DR. GANDHI: "*You sound like Majnu in search of his lost love ... Laila ... roaming restlessly ... feeling worthless ... senseless*"

JINEN: "*This is the state of my life ... my personal feelings ... why can't you or anyone else understand?*"

DR. GANDHI: "*Jinen, I have known you from the day you were born ... you are more than a son to me as I watched you grow into a young man ... I agree what happened to you is* *terrible ... senseless ... but, trying to commit suicide is not the way out ... Think of the devastation and misery you will give to your aging parents..."*

JINEN: (Weeping in agony) "*I no longer have parents ... my father disowned me when I told him I was marrying my beloved Zarina...*"

DR. GANDHI: "*No matter ... That is all in the past ... Your parents will always be your parents...*"

JINEN: (Outraged by Dr. Gandhi's words) "*That bond no longer exists...*"

DR. GANDHI: "*Don't sound so bitter...*"

JINEN (Silently shakes his head)

DR. GANDHI: "*They are outside ... waiting to see you...*"

JINEN: (Begging) "*Please, Dr. Uncle - I do not want to see them ... no one ... Nobody...*"

DR. GANDHI: "*They are your parents ... they are very concerned ... They want to see you...*"

JINEN: (Agitated and hysterical weeping) "*I want to see no one ... Especially them..*"

DR. GANDHI: "*As you wish, Jinen ... I felt sure they could help you to recover...*"

JINEN: (becoming more hysterical, pleading) "*Please, Dr. Uncle, please ... I do not wish to see them...*"

DR. GANDHI: "*Okay, okay, son... calm yourself. You need to clear your head ... your body needs rest...*"

JINEN: "*Yes, my aching body ... my throbbing head ... needs to rest forever ... That is how I feel...*"

DR. GANDHI: "*Jinen, do not give up to utter despair ... think positively ... the police are still searching for the killer. At this stage, I would advise you to talk with a psychiatrist to help you pass this crisis ... it is very traumatic for a young man...*"

JINEN: "*Dr. Gandhiji, no ... no psychiatrist ... please I want to be left along ... to think in peace...*"

DR. GANDHI: "*Then, promise me that you will not try anything irrationally,*"

JINEN: "*I refuse to make any promises...*"

DR. GANDHI: "*Well, at least try...*"

JINEN (Lying in bed ... turns over, his face in the pillow ... weeping)

Part 7

SCENES - Dr.Gandhi coming out of the ICU greeting Jinen's parents in the waiting room, he is very solemn and ill at ease.

DHIRAJLAL: "*Gandhiji, how is Jinen ... What is happening....*"

DR. GANDHI: "*He needs close observation for the next 24 hours. He is still very depressed ... under the circumstances but, he is out of danger for the present.*"

SHARDA: "*My poor son, is he all right?*"

DR. GANDHI: "*Mentally he is devastated ... Physically he needs quiet ... peace ... silence...*"

SHARDA: "*Can we see Jinen please?*"

DR. GANDHI: "*Not yet ... He is...*"

SHARDA: "*Please, he is our son ... please we need to see him...*"

DR. GANDHI: "*He does not want to see either of you ... right now. No one. We have to give him ... time...*"

SHARDA: (Shock look on her face, she turns to her husband) "*Why does Jinen not want to see us? ... What have we done? Please ... I must see my son...*"

DHIRAJLAL: (Silently standing and looking at Dr. Gandhi, holds his wife back as she advances to the door...)

DR. GANDHI: "*Shardaben, I think Jinen is in shock from what has happened. He is hurting deeply. It will not be wise for you both to see him. I cannot leave him alone for long. We need to let him rest ... sleep and...*"

SHARDA: "*But we are his family, his flesh and blood...*"

DR. GANDHI: "*Precisely, for that reason ... You both caused a great tension for him ... Let us not push him away any further from you guys...*"

SHARDA: "*But Doctor, which family does not have its moments of tensions? Our son needs us...*"

DR. GANDHI: "*Bhabhi (sister-in-law) Not right now ... Let him rest ... think things out ... He refused to see you both. You're going into his room, without his permission will put more stress on his unstable mind and then ... you may loose him forever...*"

SHARDA: "*I am his mother... he cannot break that bond. Maybe, we made a mistake in our dealing with Zarina. I will make him understand that all is forgiven.*"

DHIRAJLAL: "*Sharda, don't get so emotional. Listen to what the doctor is telling us, he is our friend...*"

DR. GANDHI: *"At this stage, Jinen needs to weather the storm alone. He needs time to recover in mind and spirit ... Give him that time..."*

DHIRAJLAL: "*Sharda, the doctor is right ... We should leave Jinen alone for the present. Let us not add fuel to the fire...*"

SHARDA: "*What are you saying?... Fuel to the fire ... You disowned him ... and look what happened ... Do you have no feelings for your son?*"

DHIRAJLAL: "*Please understand... I know he is your child and he needs you ... but we must have patience... we need to step back for his sake. Dr. Gandhi says, Jinen does not want to see us ... so we must wait...*"

SHARDA: *"What is this?... he is your child... And not your son?"*

DHIRAJLAL: "*Sharda, if you want to go in and see him, then go ahead. But I will not come in with you...*"

SHARDA: "*If we go in together, what can happen, he will refuse to see us...*"

DR. GANDHI: "*Bhabhi that is exactly what Jinen has told me... He refuses to see you both..*"

DHIRAJLAL: "*Then, Sharda, you go ahead alone*" (He turns to Dr. Gandhi, and walks ahead of his wife) *"Please keep us informed of his conditions."* (He stops and turns to his wife) *"Sharda let us go..."*

DR. GANDHI: *"Please think of your son's condition..."*

SHARDA: "*You men are all alike ... I will wait for a day or two. No more ... I want to see my son...*"

DR. GANDHI: "*Thank you Bhabhi ... You both have made a wise decision. I am sure, by the time Jinen will come to terms with reality, he will need you both to give him your love and support...*"

Part 8

SCENES - Later next day ... Dr. Gandhi is in the ICU with Jinen

DR. GANDHI: "*Jinen, How do you feel today ... any better?*"

JINEN: "*Numb ... both mentally and physically...*"

DR. GANDHI: "*Son, life is a very precious existence... and no one in their right mind should throw it all away... You need to take care of it...*"

JINEN: "*I understand what you are trying to say ... but I failed to take care of and protect my Zarina ... She was my life...*"

DR. GANDHI: "*I understand your grief ... Your loss cannot be replaced. I also know that your parents regret their harsh decision. They are repenting...*"

JINEN: "*I very much doubt it ... my parents are a different breed of human beings....*"

DR. GANDHI: "*What makes you say that?*"

JINEN: "*I am sure my father told you the whole story. You both are very close. He must be happy to hear that Zarina's is dead and....*"

DR. GANDHI: "*What about Zarina's parents?*"

JINEN: "*Her father was here a while ago. I could not face him. How can I console them? I robbed them of their daughter. I ruined their happiness...*"

DR. GANDHI: "*Did Zarina's father know that you both were getting married?*"

JINEN: "*That was my mistake. After what happened to us meeting my parents, I forced Zarina not to say anything to her parents, until after our wedding. So that we did not have to go through the drama and disappointment again...*"

DR. GANDHI: "*Oh, I see ... Her father must have been so confused and traumatized...*"

JINEN: "*Yes, Zarina's parents ... her father ... heard the story from strangers ... the police ... I am the sinner, I took away the only daughter he had*" (Starts to weep)

DR. GANDHI: (Sits on Jinen bed) "*Take a hold of yourself, Jinen...*"

JINEN: "*Zarina's parents... I could see it in their eyes ... they will never forgive me for the death of their daughter.*"

DR. GANDHI: "*But her father came to see you...*"

JINEN: "*He is a saint ... he and his family. They helped me bury Zarina and told me that they would have supported the marriage. How stupid of me to judge them with my own parents. Her father told me how much he loved his daughter and he only cared for her happiness. And here I was, telling her to forget it and not ask for her parent's permission. How could I have been so inconsiderate of not knowing the difference?*"

DR. GANDHI: "*Jinen, always remember, your parents would have come around ... they would have understood in time... Time is a great healer for the mistakes we humans make...*"

JINEN: "*It's too late to regret what we all have done... the words ... the denial of acceptance in the name of love...*"

DR. GANDHI: "*Remember, you and your parents are as much to blame... We all make mistakes, we are but human. You never once warned them about Zarina's love in your life. You must pull yourself and cope with the future by facing the truth ... circumstances that are forcing you to become brave. There is still the question of finding who is the killer? It is important to know who is behind all this senseless killing and devastation of human souls...*"

JINEN: (He shakes his head, with a determined look in his eyes) "*More than life itself, I want to know who dared to target my Zarina... She was completely innocent of all my impatient doings... May God forgive me...*"

DR. GANDHI: "*Jinen, the head nurse told me that you were interviewed by two detectives in your room...?*"

JINEN: "*Yes... yes... we spoke... they wanted more information, as they have no leads of the shooting ... Can you imagine,* *absolutely no leads ... who could have done this horrendous crime?"*

DR. GANDHI: *"It is such an outrageous act ... unthinkable ...who could have ever thought of it? I am sure they will find the shooter and punish him..."*

JINEN: (Tears welling from his eyes, his lips quivering, uncontrollable) *"Dr. Uncle, they must find the killer ... like the saying goes, from your mouth to God's ears ... His will be done..."*

DR. GANDHI: "*Come, you must lie down and rest ... Tomorrow is another day ... where new light will be shed on the truth and reality..."*

JINEN: "*I appreciate your good will and encouragement of thought, but ... everything that has happened seems so senseless and futile..."*

DR. GANDHI: "*No, no, come my son ... rest ... sleep is the only savior ... Good night..."*

JINEN: "*Hmm, may be ... may be not ... I dread to close my eyes ... all I see is Zarina lying in my arms smiling innocently with a bullet wound in her head ... How can I forget ... it has been my nightmare for the past few days ... But sleep I must to get my mind rested from all this confusion..."*

NEXT DAY (Nurse Florence Knightingile is seen running down the hospital corridor to Dr. Gandhi's Office...)

NURSE FLORENCE KNIGHTINGILE: *"Dr. Gandhi ... Dr. Gandhi"*

DR. GANDHI: "*Flo, Do you need me? What is the matter? Calm yourself...*"

NURSE FLORENCE: "*Your patient ... in Room 345 has gone ... disappeared ...I cannot find him anywhere...*"

DR. GANDHI: "*Which patient ... Disappeared? He may be in the toilet?*"

NURSE FLORENCE: "*He is no where ... I have looked everywhere ... The young man who tried to commit suicide ...Jinen.*"

DR. GANDHI: "*You mean Jinen?*"

NURSE FLORENCE: "*Yes ... that patient ... I went in his room to give him his medicine and he was gone ... no sign of his clothes in the closet ...shoes ... nothing*"

DR. GANDHI: "*Last night, I left him in the ICU...*"

NURSE FLORENCE: "*Yes, he was not moved ... he should have been lying in bed resting...*"

DR. GANDHI: "*Then how did he escape ... Is he in the waiting room? He is not strong enough to leave the hospital...*"

NURSE FLORENCE: "*I checked with the guard ... he was requested by a young man ... to walk outside in the garden...*"

DR. GANDHI: "*He could not have been feeling better ... He was too weak with all the pills we pumped out of his stomach last night...*"

NURSE FLORENCE: "*I know, I know ... It looks like he got out of his bed, put on his clothes, shoes and went left the ICU...*"

DR. GANDHI: "*... With his IV pole...*"

NURSE FLORENCE: "*Yes ... I have been looking for him over ten minutes, and found his IV pole in the visitors' lounge ... He has gone...*"

DR. GANDHI: "*What about the security at the entrance of the hospital?*"

NURSE FLORENCE: "*I phoned to find out, but nobody recollects a patient leaving ... He tricked everyone by walking out as a regular visitor...*"

Jinen's parents are seen walking in the corridor. They see Dr. Gandhi and wave to him.

DR. GANDHI: (to Nurse Florence) "*Jinen's parents have arrived ... they want to see him ... what shall I say to them?*"

SHARDA: "*Good morning, doctor ... how are you today...*"

DR GANDHI: "*Bhabhi ... There is nothing good ... about today...*"

DHIRAJLAL: "*Doctor Gandhi, my friend, why are you in such a disturbed mood ... Did you argue with your wife this morning*" (teasing the doctor)

DR. GANDHI: "*Please ...don't blame my poor wife ... I have some bad news for you...*"

DHIRAJLAL: "*Bad news ...You look so serious today ... What happened to your smiling face? Things could not be that bad...*"

SHARDA: "*So, tell me, tell me ... how is our beloved son, Jinen coming along ... Can I see him, please ... We can go into his room...*"

DR. GANDHI: "*That is the bad news...*"

SHARDA: "*My Jinen ... has anything happened since yesterday....*"

DR. GANDHI: "*Yes ... there is a problem...*"

DHIRAJLAL: "*Have there been some complications to his health since yesterday?*"

SHARDA: "*Oh, my God ... please tell us what has happened.... To my Jinen*"

DR. GANDHI: (Clears his throat and takes Jinen's mother's hand...) "*Now, you must take this news calmly...*"

SHARDA: "*What news? What are you talking about ... my Jinen?*"

DHIRAJLAL: "*Oh, just tell her what is wrong...*"

DR. GANDHI: "*There is nothing wrong ... nothing ... He is simply not here...*"

DHIRAJLAL & SHARDA: (Echo together) "*Not here ... then where ... where have they taken him...*"

DR. GANDHI: "*Please calm yourselves ... He left the hospital without telling anyone ... He just walked out of the entrance door...*"

SHARDA: "*But how can this happen? In a hospital...*"

DHIRAJLAL: "*... They are supposed to take care of the patient's safety ... Not allow sick patients to walk out...*"

DR GANDHI: "*Well, a hospital is not a prison ... and Jinen is not a child who wandered off ... He is a grown man ... Still I am sorry for what happened...*"

SHARDA: (Her lips quiver as she starts to weep...) "*Has he gone away ... forever ... I will never see him again?*"

DHIRAJLAL: "*Stop weeping; don't talk like that...*"

DR. GANDHI: "*I am sure Jinen is OK ... He has a strong head on his shoulders ... He needs time to think...*"

SHARDA: (Looking at her husband helplessly...) "*I do not feel OK ... Jinen is my only son ... our only child. I wish we could have seen him ... met him yesterday.*"

DHIRAJLAL: "*We should not have listened to you yesterday Dr. Gandhi*"

SHARDA: "*Yes, yes, why did we listen to you ... oh, why oh why!*"

DR. GANDHI: "*Bhabhiji, please don't blame yourself ... Jinen wanted to be alone ... We will find him ... He is a good kid and very responsible...*"

SHARDA: "*He may be gone home to meet us ... come, hurry up ... let us leave and return home*"

DHIRAJLAL: "*Dr. Gandhiji, I am worried, you don't think he will try to commit ... try to ... again ... May be, he went home...*"

DR. GANDHI: (Placing his hand on the father's mouth...) "*Don't even think about it ... Just keep those thoughts out of your mind....*"

PART 9

In a distance is the landscape of Siddhi Challum - the Jain Ashram in NJ, Jinen is sitting against the tree, his eyes are closed, his hair is rugged untidily as though he was sleeping, his motor bike is lying in the grass, it is in the early hours of dawn. The sunrise starts to peak into the sky. In a distance, a solitary figure of a Jain monk, draped in a white cloth appears. As he comes closer, a small square piece of white cloth is draped across his mouth, tied with two strings to the back of his head. He moves carefully, treading the ground with care, with a peacock feather, sweeping away any possible living being lying in his footpath. He reaches where Jinen is seated.

CHANDRAMOHAN/MONK: *"Jai Jinendra ... what are you doing out here in the open air at this hour of dawn...?"*

JINEN: (His bloodshot eyes are hollowed with dark circles, his looks at the monk in a dazed state of mind - of a man who has not slept or eaten for days) *"Swamiji, I need to be out in the open ... I am beyond help..."*

CHANDRAMOHAN: *"Yes, you look like a man completely lost within and without ... as though you tried committing Sallekhana..."*

JINEN: "*Yes, Sallekhana ... the voluntary termination of one's life ... equivalent to modern day committing suicide...*"

CHANDRAMOHAN: (Stands still and stares into the young man's eyes) "*Suicide is committed on a sudden impulse ... normally due to misfortunes of one's own making...*"

JINEN: "*Yes, Swamiji ... It resulted out of mental weakness ... and external pressures of circumstances...*"

CHANDRAMOHAN: "*The only way man can transform himself is through penance and resolve. Come with me, you must eat something...*"

JINEN: "*Please don't worry about me...*"

CHANDRAMOHAN: "*You look like you need to have some hot tea ... tired and hungry...*"

JINEN: "*Desires of the body but not of the mind.... Memories that keep returning....*"

CHANDRAMOHAN: "*You are upset about something ... deeply disturbed...*"

JINEN: (Realizes he is talking to a stranger...) "*That's none of your business...*"

CHANDRAMOHAN: "*I agree ... But first you must take care ... and strengthen your body ... then your memories and then the soul within you...*"

JINEN: (Voice annoyed at the monk's humility) *"Please stop preaching to me ... It is impossible for me to change what happened to me..."*

CHANDRAMOHAN: *"My son, please understand - one reality. No one can change a man with preaching. Seasons can be changed, nature can be changed, but it is not easy to change a man. If man is to be changed, there is a whole process of change that must be undertaken ... some times it takes a whole life time ... "*

JINEN: *"Change is not impossible, but it is not easy nor simple either."*

CHANDRAMOHAN: *"Do you think it was easy to become a monk? No, my son ... Jain Dharma is tough ... a religion based on facts and logic. It is teachings and preaching of God Mahavir that are badly needed in this modern world. I am not preaching ... just trying to make conversation ... I am concerned about your well being..."*

JINEN: *"Please ... STOP..."*

CHANDRAMOHAN: *"I will stop ... if you come inside the Ashram and have something to eat ... has some rest."*

JINEN: *"Then what ... live in the misery of my memories...?"*

CHANDRAMOHAN: *"Well, son, that is up to you ... but you coming inside the Ashram will make me happy..."*

JINEN: (Quietly rises...)

CHANDRAMOHAN: *"If you refuse my request, it will sadden me ... So please have mercy on me and accompany me into the Ashram ... I ask for nothing more"*

JINEN: stands up... (Reluctantly, Jinen follows the Monk into the Ashram)

Later that morning.

CHANDRAMOHAN: (Sees Jinen seated, sipping a hot cup of tea...) *"I hope the cup of tea helped you to ease your mind and I hope you got at least forty winks of sleep..."*

JINEN: (Smiles gently at the Monk's concern) *"Yes, I dozed off..."*

CHANDRAMOHAN: *"You need guidance and help to put your problems to rest..."*

JINEN: *"Are you a mind reader? You are so correct, I am in mental agony..."*

CHANDRAMOHAN: *"That is so obvious ... just looking into your eyes ... I feel your spiritual agony..."*

JINEN: *"I am suffering with many great problems ... both mentally and physically..."*

CHANDRAMOHAN: *"Of course you are ... son..."*

JINEN: *"Thanks for understanding ... my own father was unable to comprehend what I was saying..."*

CHANDRAMOHAN: *"It is a father's duty to protect his child..."*

JINEN: *"But I am no longer a child ... I am ... I was a man with responsibilities..."*

CHANDRAMOHAN: *"Yes, that is very important to understand..."*

JINEN: *"There was no understanding ... I was talking to a blank wall ... My father's voice condemning every word of explanation ... love..."*

CHANDRAMOHAN: *"At this stage, you need to change your direction of thinking ... Change the thoughts as they come into your mind ... Think of your father's kindness..."*

JINEN: *"No, there is no understanding and kindness in his voice..."*

CHANDRAMOHAN: *"Then think of the kindness within you ...and forgiveness ... forgive your father ... that is a positive thought..."*

JINEN: *"Impossible ... I can't forgive my father or mother ... Today, there is no meaning to my life ... You will never understand my state of mind..."*

CHANDRAMOHAN: *"Perhaps you are correct ... But every living being on earth has a meaning to life ... We are here for a reason ... which we question repeatedly through life ... but first try and remove all this sorrow and self pity..."*

JINEN: *"Sorrow ... I no longer want to live with this aching sorrow in my heart..."*

CHANDRAMOHAN: *"There is a solution ... If you no longer value your existence on earth ... then learn to live for others..."*

JINEN: *"Live for others...?"*

CHANDRAMOHAN: *"Yes, share your life for another ... there are others who will benefit..."*

JINEN: *"All these words are loaded ... It is too much to think about now..."*

CHANDRAMOHAN: *"You are correct ... I agree ...Take your time and roam freely on the grounds ... It is important to see through your problems and mental anguish"*

JINEN: *"Guruji, thank you for insisting that I take some food and shelter ... I feel my nerves calming ... the throbbing of my brains lightening..."*

CHANDRAMOHAN: *"Whatever you decide ... it is important to rest the mind ... invite new thoughts from the divine spirit within you..."*

JINEN: *"Yes ... There is such natural beauty in the Ashram gardens ... I need to walk among the trees ... play like a child ... my feet naked feeling the grass..."*

CHANDRAMOHAN: *"Son, life is made of simple tasks, but living it, becomes complicated ... Place your faith in the divine power of Mahavirji..."*

JINEN: *"These past few ... days ... hours ... have been terrible ... the loss of my love, my very breath of existence ... miscalculating my parents behavior..."*

CHANDRAMOHAN: *"I feel your loss ... your overwhelming sorrow ... Would you like to talk about her...?"*

JINEN: *"There is nothing to say any more ... my life, my love, my wife ... all gone with one shot ... as she lay in my arms..."*

CHANDRAMOHAN: *"What was her name?"*

JINEN: (Starts to weep helplessly...) *"Zarina ... Zarina..."*

CHANDRAMOHAN: (Unable to share the agony of the young man ... He sits next to him) *"Love is a great equalizer ... You shared a great love together..."*

JINEN: *"We were two people as one ... one soul, one body ... where our love was concerned ... How can I convince you...? I was unable to do it with my parents ... who completely rejected our love..."*

CHANDRAMOHAN: *"Your words show me what you felt ... You must calm yourself ... What did you mean by ... gone with one shot?"*

JINEN: *"Oh, my God, how can I ... within one brief second ... there was a bullet shot through her head ... she looked at me smiling ... thanking me for our love..."*

CHANDRAMOHAN: *"Oh, oh, I see what you are going through ... This is a terrible tragedy ... it is written all over in the newspapers in the last few days."*

JINEN: *"Swamiji, help me ... my Zarina has gone ... gone ... her life ended with one meaningless shot..."*

CHANDRAMOHAN: *"Forgive me, my son, I opened your wound ... I am sorry I asked ... You must take control of your life..."*

JINEN: *"All I feel is dead ... inside and out ... I cannot bear to look into the light ... yet I see her smiling face everywhere ... I no longer want to live..."*

CHANDRAMOHAN: *"Live you must ... through the greatest of sorrow, we have endured ... You must conquer your grief ... it will take time..."*

JINEN: *"It seems impossible ... how can I conquer this haunting grief ... it terrifies me to think about it ... Each moment is stamped on my forehead...?"*

CHANDRAMOHAN: *"You are correct. Nothing I say or do can take this agony away ... I feel for you ... and all I can do is pray for strength ... so that you are given the strength from the divine powers to overcome all this terrible burden of unhappiness ... You may think I do not understand your pain ... but we must pray together ... You will only find peace in prayer ... Come with me..."*

JINEN: *"Prayer ... is prayer my only solution? ... Will I be able to forget all this agony? ... And"*

CHANDRAMOHAN: *"Forgive yourself, as Zarina would have wanted you to forgive yourself for the accident."*

JINEN: *"Yes, yes ... you are right ... I need to forgive..."*

CHANDRAMOHAN: *"... Pray and ask for her forgiveness so her spirit may rest in peace..."*

JINEN: *"So I may feel forgiveness ... not this terrible agonizing guilt for our love and marriage vows..."*

Jinen closing his eyes, falling asleep, in a dream saw his mother and heard voices.

Q: *What is God?*

A: *You, others, and I are souls suffering the bondage of karma. The soul's existence in its natural state that is in freedom of karma and purely as the atman that it is Ishvar (God). That which has the aishvarya (presence of knowledge), etc. maybe described as Ishvar. This Ishvarhood is the natural state of the atman (soul), which is not revealed when it is engaged in karma, when it is not its real nature and fixes its attention on itself, then alone do omniscience, power, etc. manifest themselves in it and we can see nothing among all the objects in the universe with greater power than the atman's. It is therefore my positive believe that Ishvar is another name for atman and does not signify a different being of greater power.*

Q: *What is Moksha?*

A: *While the atman (soul) is in the state of ignorance characterized by anger, etc. it is under the bondage of the body, and complete cessation such a state, deliverance from it, is described by seers as moksha (means nirvana). A little reflection shows this to be logical and convincing.*

Q: *What will finally happen to this world?*

A: *It does not seem rationally possible to me that all souls will attain absolute moksha or that the world will perish completely. It is likely to continue to exist forever in the same state as the present. Some expects of it may under go transformation and almost disappear and another may grow. Such is the nature of the world that, if there is growth in one sphere, there is decline in another. Having regard to this fact and after deep reflection, it seems impossible to me that this world will perish completely. By "world" we do not mean this earth only.*

Jinen awaken from his dream saw the monk standing in front of him.

Monk & Jinen are seen praying, lips moving, the bell resounding in the temple and then they move into the Ashram gardens.

CHANDRAMOHAN: *"It is my humble request that you stay at the Ashram for as long as it takes to bring comfort to your soul. Remember, she wants you to live, it is no use to throw your life* away..."

JINEN: *"But to keep living ... I need to have a reason..."*

CHANDRAMOHAN: *"Jinen, you were put on this earth for a reason. That, I am sure. We spend a lifetime questioning that reason, when it is right in our faces..."*

JINEN: *"Guruji, your reason was and is to comfort ... do seva (service) for other people..."*

CHANDRAMOHAN: *"Stay a while ... You are thinking like a man with a passionate heart ... look beyond the heart*

... communicate with your inner soul ... you will find your answer..."

JINEN: *"Inner soul ... loving Zarina we were one soul..."*

CHANDRAMOHAN: *"Yes, so try and communicate with that soul ... It is*

something that you can learn..."

JINEN: *"Learn? I need to think this thought through..."*

CHANDRAMOHAN: *"Think in a silence first ... You can always find me here ... Now let us go and have breakfast in the dinning hall. Have you breathed in the fresh air ... look at the sunshine ... even though the window is howling, the birds are chirping and life is awakening to a new day..."*

JINEN: *"All this is meaningless..."*

CHANDRAMOHAN: *"You are stepping into a new day ... as though into a new life ... there is new meaning for your thoughts ... forgiveness ... Think seriously on those words..."*

JINEN: *"Yes, you are right ... I cannot forgive myself for what happened to Zarina ... There lives may torment my soul..."*

CHANDRAMOHAN: *"There is a way to heal that tormented soul ... it is possible ... all you have to do is reach out..."*

JINEN - DREAM SEQUENCE - Jinen is seen against the Siddhi Challum landscape walking into outer space. (Theme Song begins again)

Whose love? This is all I think.
Our love is in the village of the heart.
He will not see me stopping here ever.
To watch our true love fill up with happiness.
Our little horse love may think it queer.
To stop without a secret love farmhouse near.
Between two lovers will be the "STORM" of the century.
He gives harness bells shake.
To ask if there is some error.
The only other skies that sweep.
Of stormy wind and downy flake.
The two lovers are great, sparkling soul.
But I have committed to keep.
And miles to fly in ending love.
Before I sleep…
Before I sleep…

ZARINA: (Echoes of her voice ... as though from the sky...) *"Jinen ... Jinen, JINEN, my love..."*

JINEN: *"Zarina, my love.. Is that you?"*

ZARINA: *"Yes ... it is me ...my love..."*

JINEN: *"Where ... where are you?"*

ZARINA: (Stands before Jinen and takes his hand ... though in a dream) *"Have you already forgotten how I looked?"*

JINEN: *"No, no, never in a hundred life times ... But why can't I see you more clearly ... more real..."*

ZARINA: *"Open your heart and your soul ... they are the windows of your eyes..."*

JINEN: (Close-up ... opens his eyes and stares Zarina Full Face) *"So you are here ... really here ... holding my hand and loving me ... don't ever let go..."*

ZARINA: *"No, never let go of my hand..."*

JINEN: (Close-up of both their hands entwined together. They embrace and kiss)

JINEN: *"Zarina, I miss you so much ... every single moment ... I think only of you..."*

ZARINA: *"I cannot breath without you ... Every second I wonder where you are ... what you are doing..."*

JINEN: *"Never let me go ... I thought I had lost you forever."*

ZARINA: *"That will never be ... We belong to each other ... we are one soul ... one body..."*

JINEN: *"Yes, we belong to each other ... one soul, one body ... nothing will ever keep us apart..."*

ZARINA: *"Always remember ... look deep in your heart and I will never leave you..."*

JINEN: *"Promise? If you even think of leaving me for one moment ... the thought depresses me..."*

ZARINA: *"Our love is exceptional and forever ... nothing will ever change that thought ... always remember ... nothing will change our love..."*

JINEN: *"You know you are the only woman for me ... there will never be another Zarina in my life..."*

ZARINA: *"It is important for us to share our lives with others ... We must live and care for others as we live and care, refreshing for our love together each day..."*

JINEN: *"No, Zarina, we don't need others ...You are the only one I love and care for ... no one else. I sacrificed my family and my father for our love..."*

ZARINA: *"Our love is more than any sacrifice ... but you have to understand that your father's love is like our love ... We care ... Open your heart and mind and share this great love we feel for each other ... so all people can recognize what it means to really love ... and they will feel fulfilled also..."*

JINEN: *"Now what are you talking about? I don't understand."*

ZARINA: *"You will understand ... Love takes time ... patience ... tolerance of others ... respect..."*

JINEN: *"Zarina, we need no one except each other..."*

ZARINA: *"Yes, but to expand our love ... we need to share it with the people we love ... your parents ... my parents ... You need humility and forgiveness"*

JINEN: *"Now, what are you talking about humility and forgiveness?"*

ZARINA: *"Think of your parents ... my parents ... our lives ... we share a beautiful happiness ... a once in a lifetime love affair ...remember disco dance? I am a dancer"*

JINEN: *"True, so true ... yes ... I must forgive my father and mother ... and myself ...take me with you to dance...."*

Monk taps Jinen on the shoulder, he turns around to face him, and his face has been transformed into humility

CHANDRAMOHAN/MONK: *"My son, who were you talking to..."*

JINEN: *"My Zarina ... she was here ... I was talking to her about forgiveness and humility...I wanted to dance with her... but she left...she has gone...".*

CHANDRAMOHAN: *"Yes, I am sure she was here ... "*

JINEN: (Trying to convince the Monk...) *"Guruji, I promise you she stood here ... where did she go..."*

CHANDRAMOHAN: *"Jinen, if you love each other so much, she will never leave your side ... She will always be with you ... in your heart ... and part of your soul..."*

JINEN: *"Yes ... you are right ... We will always have each other..."*

CHANDRAMOHAN: *"Remember, the human body dies, but the soul lives on ... Every time you need her, she will be there ... Just close your eyes..."*

JINEN: *"She said ... time will heal the physical emptiness and pain"*

CHANDRAMOHAN: *"Yes, take one step at a time ... Do not ignore your own existence ... seek and you will find, knock*

and the door will be open, enter and your search for salvation begins..."

Both men are seen against the Siddhi Chalam landscape. It is snowing and time is passing by. Show the season as the passage of months, years.

FLASH BACK

Part 10

SCENES: In a motel room. Zarina and Jinen are lying in bed kissing each other passionately.

JINEN: *"Do you remember the first night we met ...in the storm ... the thunder and lightening..."*

ZARINA: *"And there you were ... my knight and shinning arm ... seated on the Harley Davidson ... Do you think it was love at first sight...?"*

JINEN: *"I could not take my eyes off you ... you looked so helpless ... so beautiful..."*

ZARINA: *"Excuse me, I was not helpless ... I had some spray where I would have protected myself..."*

JINEN: *"Oh, Oh ... so she did not need her knight to save her from the lousy drunk?"*

ZARINA: *"Gosh, Jinen, you scared me ... I cannot even think what would have happened, if you hadn't rescued me..."*

JINEN: (Laughing and singing) *"Rescue me when I am down..."*

ZARINA: *"Okay, Darling... I confess ... I don't know what I would have done ... I know that I owe you my life..."*

JINEN: *"I am the savior of your fate ... you are my destiny ... nothing will ever change that ... Oh, God - how much I love you..."*

ZARINA: *"Shhh ...People will hear us ... with these cardboard walls..."*

JINEN: *"Let the whole world know how much I love you my love ... I want to shout it from the highest mountain"*

ZARINA: *"You mean, the Himalayas...?"*

JINEN: *"Don't disturb my thought ...I want to shout out aloud: ZARINA BANU, I love you with all my heart, with all my strength..."*

ZARINA: *"With all my soul...?"*

JINEN: *"You know ... we are soul mates ... we must have known each other in another life..."*

ZARINA: *"May be, I was Cleopatra and you were my great lover - Caesar or Marcus"*

JINEN: *"Let's keep to the greater classical lovers ... Laila and Majnu ... Romeo and Juliet..."*

ZARINA: *"Do you really love me that much?"*

JINEN: *"Yes Zari ... Why do you doubt my love for a moment?"*

ZARINA: *"Just asked ... need to be convinced by Romeo or whoever...?"*

JINEN: *"Zarina my love, never question the great love I have for you ... you are my first and only true love..."*

ZARINA: (Teasing...) *"First and only ... what if you get tired of me ... I saw how you were looking at all those other girls..."*

JINEN: *"What other girls? My eyes are only for you..."*

ZARINA: (Teasing...) *"It is good that I am not a very jealous woman ... otherwise, I would have..."*

JINEN: *"What would you have? What would I have? You have no worries ... I am yours and yours alone..."*

ZARINA: *"Well ... I wanted to tell you something, which may raise a flag of caution..."*

JINEN: *"Now, don't be party poppers ... why all this doubt about our love ... don't you trust me?"*

ZARINA: *"There is no doubt about our love ... my feelings ... I am truly blessed by meeting you, my love..."*

JINEN: *"Never ever doubt my love for you ... Because I am so happy to be by your side ...I forgive you ... but next time, I may not be this kind."*

ZARINA: *"I thank you for your forgiveness and did you say kindness? That I can accept ... but what will you ... how will you react to my news...?"*

JINEN: *"What news? Have you got a promotion at work? I know how hard you work..."*

ZARINA: *"Thanks. I am so glad you understand ... but I am trying to get into this royal mood, my majesty ... Badshahji (king)"*

JINEN: *"Yes, my Begumji (queen) ... my wish is your command ... You have made me the happiest man in the world and I am obliged to grant you one wish..."*

ZARINA: (Getting up from the bed her eyes moving restlessly as she has something to confess) *"Wow, I get one whole wish."*

JINEN: *"As I have gifted myself to you completely from the day we met ... I would now like to grant you one wish, my beautiful Begumji ... Wish for anything..."*

ZARINA: *"One wish, one wish ... what will that be ... I wish...."*

JINEN: *"Yes, what it is that you wish for the most in the world?"*

ZARINA: *"I wish we ... Well, besides the wish ... I need to give you some news..."*

JINEN: *"News? What news is more important than a wish I can't grant you?"*

ZARINA: (She blurts out annoyed with herself) *"You guys are all the same ... impatient ... refusing to share news"*

JINEN: *"Guys ... all the same ... This is me ... Jinen ... you are talking to ... I am only one of a kind..."*

ZARINA: *"Yes, I know ...But I need to say you love me..."*

JINEN: *"Oh, my god, Zarina ... how many times do you need to hear me say that...? Yesterday you told me to stop."*

ZARINA: *"Yes, yes ... but I need you to convince me that with your love ... we can walk through fire..."*

JINEN: (Gets off the bed and encircles Zarina in his arms) *"Of course, the love I feel for you ... There is no man on earth that can make me feel like you do ... Yes, I will walk through fire for our love ... Are you convinced?"*

ZARINA: (Speaks sharply, biting her lips...) *"With this great love ... you got what you wanted..."*

JINEN: (He stares into her eyes) *"Zarina ... what is the matter?"*

ZARINA:*"I am sorry ... you are always joking and teasing me..."*

JINEN: *"If I have offended you in any way ... just tell me ... I know nothing stopped us from loving each other ... but you wanted it too..."*

ZARINA: *"Because I love you as much as you love me, Jinen..."*

JINEN: *"So, what did you mean by ... you got what you wanted? Please never doubt my intentions. I am yours forever. You are my life..."*

ZARINA: *"Hey, let's stop all this talk ... Your love makes me so happy..."*

JINEN: *"True, true ... Do you know where I am taking you this evening?"*

ZARINA: *"I thought you forgot ... this is our third month meeting each other ... anniversary ... Tell me, tell me ... where?"*

JINEN: *"First you have to give me one of those passionate kisses ... "*

ZARINA: (Kisses Jinen really passionately ...her eyes closed ... his eyes opened in surprise) *"Where will you take me tonight for our anniversary?"*

JINEN: *"To your favorite Broadway play and then dinner at Bay Leaf ... my friend Kevin with his Broadway contacts, helped me to get tickets..."*

ZARINA: *"I like Kevin ... he always comes through for you ... he is a good friend..."*

JINEN: *"He and his girlfriend Martha will come to the theater with us ... He says he is going steady with her..."*

ZARINA: *"This is awesome ... you think of everything ... I hope you will be the same man after you hear my news..."*

JINEN: *"You know how dumb I can be ... do tell us the news?"*

ZARINA: (Hesitating...)*"May be, after we tie the knot..."*

JINEN: *"Hey, hey, hey ... you are jumping ahead of time ... We have to tell my parents first..."*

ZARINA: *"Yes, that's what you want..."*

JINEN: *"Remember, your every wish is my command..."*

ZARINA: *"That's my boy ... that's my great love..."*

Part 11

SCENES: Hospital scene. Close up of Dr. Gandhi as he is seen cutting and removing bandages from the face of a patient whose back is to him. Music will start to create suspense around the presence of the stranger as if who is this new character that entered the film? He must bear no resemblance to Jinen's father. Both the conversation and the music will dramatize the presence of this mysterious stranger who has undergone a major plastic surgery under the skilled hands of Dr. Gandhi - where the filmgoers have the idea that he may be a gangster/businessman who is trying to escape from the police?

Song.

Hey brave guy, it's a challenge for you
To adjust to a new life
You are born with a fist
Oh Dear God, You lost everything,
But still hope to be divine
I know masking your face, body, and soul
It's not good to do
But you are not God
You are only human
You'll spend the rest of your life as a disciple
Accompanying your son and being happy
God may help to forgive all your past

DR. RAJIV GANDHI (PLASTIC SURGEON): (Scissors in his hand ... while a nurse assists standing next to him) *"How are you feeling? Let me know at once, if you are feeling any pain ... don't forget, you underwent major plastic surgery...?"*

PATIENT (DHIRAJLAL): (All that can be seen is his hollow eyes from behind the bandages...) *"Yes, yes, I am aware how painful the process is ... everytime the pain killing drugs evaporates, I feel the excruciating ... tingling ... raw pain..."* (Pause) *"I hope you cut deep into the burns, to give me a brand new face."*

DR. GANDHI: (Carefully cutting the gauze covering his patient's face) *"Be assured my skin specialist has done the best after your terrible 3rd degree burns ... You will not recognize yourself ... This is what you wanted?"*

DHIRAJLAL: (Talks in voice of great anxiety and impatience) *"Yes, Yes, I am worried about the face scars ... Will they disappear later?"* (Pause) *"The surgery lasted much longer than I thought ... "*

DR. GANDHI: *"Your skin was very badly burnt ... We had to use new skin from your thighs..."*

DHIRAJLAL: (Talks in a hoarse voice ... more like a Godfather gangster) *"Dr. Rajiv I know ... I endured the excruciating pains ... I must have a completely new face? A face ... no one can recognize..."*

DR. GANDHI: *"We cut deep ... and then it took weeks ... months ... for your skin to heal..."*

DHIRAJLAL: *"... And the sensations of burning and cutting off skin ... you can't image the pain..."*

DR. GANDHI: *"But you were injected with strong pain killing drugs in order to immune the skin textures."*

DHIRAJLAL: (Swallows three pills ... handed to him by the nurse) *"Forget these pills ... it hurts so badly when I swallow..."*

DR. GANDHI: *"Remember you underwent three to four surgeries ... with skin drafting that takes time to heal ... "*

DHIRAJLAL: *"I know, it was not an easy job ... but thanks in advance for taking care of me during this nightmare..."*

DR. GANDHI: *"As your doctor, I appreciate your thanks ... I hope you can understand - it seems like I am unveiling my painting as a plastic surgeon..."*

DHIRAJLAL: (His eyes watching Dr. Rajiv moving slowly and steadily unwrapping the bandages) *"It demands so much patience ... But time is of essence ... I need to leave as soon as possible..."*

DR. GANDHI: *"I need to keep a very steady hand ... one wrong move and we may peel off fresh skin ... leaving deep scars on the face..."*

DHIRAJLAL: *"Oh, We don't want that - I am paying plenty for a new face, my friend..."*

DR. GANDHI: (works on the bandages, talking with the nurse) *"Now - I hope you are ready to accept your new face ... Are you ready?"*

DHIRAJLAL: *"I have been ready from the day I came to the hospital"*

DR. GANDHI: *"Yes, I am jeopardizing my position as a doctor in this hospital by doing this favor ... Now, please, I need you to close your eyes..."*

DHIRAJLAL: *"I will remember this favor ... but it has to be done this way ... no one must know my identity..."*

DR. GANDHI: (Hands him the mirror) *"Yes, I understand ... So, let me ... what do you think about your new identity? Shocked by what you see ... Take a few moments and judge my workmanship on your face..."*

Both men whisper "Jain Stavan"{prayer song} - next shot his eyes turn and look into the mirror. There is silence.

Prayer Song.

Brotherhood Bhanjan

Maitri Bhavnu Pavitra Jarnu, Muj Haiyama Vahya Kare.
Shubh thao A Sakal Vishvanu, Avi Bhavna Nitya Rahe.
Gunthi Bharela Guni jan Dekhi, Haiyu Manu Nrutya Kare
A Santona Charan Kamal Ma, Muj Jivan Nu Arghya Rahe.
Dinhin ne Dharma Vihona, Dekhi Dilma Darda Rahe.
Karuna Bhini Ankhomathi Ashru No Subhu Shrot Vahe.
Marg Bhulela Jivan Pathikne, Marg Chindhva Ubho Rahu.
Kare Upeksha A Maragani, Toye Samta Chita Dharu.
Vira Prabhu Ni Dharma Bhavna, Haiya Sau Manav Lave.
Ver Jhr Na Pap Tyajine, Mangal Gito Sau Gave.

DHIRAJLAL: *"Wow! This is a masterpiece ... I hardly recognize myself ... you have given me a younger face with different features..."*

DR. GANDHI: (Turns to Florence, the nurse with a teasing remark) *"Well, nurse ... would you fall in love with this face?"*

DHIRAJLAL: (Humbled in embarrassment...) *"My skin looks all pinky like a baby..."*

DR. GANDHI: *"Pinky? ... The new skin will start to heal and dry ... so you won't look so pink..."*

DHIRAJLAL: *"No one ... nobody ... not one soul will recognize me ... I have no words ... except gratitude for what you have done for me..."*

DR. GANDHI: *"You can now consider yourself a new man with a new face, my friend..."*

DHIRAJLAL: *"New man, new face ... and those terrible memories of the dismal past not so long ago..."*

DR. GANDHI: *"Unfortunately, I am not a miracle worker ... I cannot erase memories of your yesterday ... but think yourself a new man for today and tomorrow..."*

DHIRAJLAL: *"Thank you, thank you ... you have done an excellent job ... I must prepare myself from today forward ... I have much to do..."*

DR. GANDHI: *"I bless you with happiness ... though I do not like the sadness in your eyes..."*

DHIRAJLAL: *"For some of us, life is not all happiness ... I need the time of day ... to pray and pay for my bad acts of karmas..."*

DR. GANDHI: (He turns to the nurse and asks her to leave the room) *"What is all this talk about bad acts of karma?"*

DHIRAJLAL: (Refuses to answer, but takes Dr. Rajiv's hand and thanks him) *"Remember, I will always be grateful for this miracle ... this great transformation, when I was in such desperate need."*

DR. GANDHI: *"Say no more ... Your circumstances were very important to me ... I always remember what and how much I love you"...*

DHIRAJLAL: *"I am sorry for forcing you ... demanding your help ... but it was very necessary..."*

DR. GANDHI: *"I know, I understand..."*

DHIRAJLAL: *"No, you have no inkling about my terrible past ... Today, you have performed a miracle ... giving me the time ... I need to make amends with people whose trust I betrayed, bringing unhappiness and misery into their lives ... If you only knew my selfish acts and what heartaches and pain I've caused..."*

SCENE changes after there is a visual collage of echoes of loud weeping, crying and voices of anger, words of abuse as though the patient has been a gangster/businessman without any forgiveness, So that the filmgoer has no indication that the patient is Jinen's father.

Part 12

SCENES: Jinen returns to the Siddhi Challum driving recklessly on his motorcycle in the gardens. There are tears in his blood shot eyes. He had returned to New York, but found Dr. Rajiv telling him that his parents had died in a car accident on the highway. It was a very tragic scene, as they were burned alive when the car blew up into flames. He was seen at the cremation, lighting the fire on his parent's pyre. Flames and more flames are seen, his face in the background looks at the loss of his father and mother.

CHANDRAMOHAN: (Seated in the temple performing prayer, then moving out into the garden, waving his peacock feature as he carefully stepped on the ground. He looks up and sees Jinen's motorcycle and sees the young man) *"Jinen ... my son ... Come, come ... have you come to pray?"*

JINEN: (Weeping uncontrollably ... unashamed) *"Guruji ... I need you to pray for me ... for my mother and my father ... for Zarina..".*

CHANDRAMOHAN: (He takes his hand and blesses Jinen on the head, while Jinen bends down to touch his feet in reverence) *"Yes, we must pray for their souls ... I heard about their tragic car accident from Dr. Rajiv ... it is a great loss for you..."*

JINEN: *"Yes, he has been phoning everyone who knew my parents..."*

CHANDRAMOHAN: *"Doctor is very worried about you..."*

JINEN: *"I know, he was a great friend to my parents ... especially my father..."*

CHANDRAMOHAN: *"It is important for you to understand. We are a small community in this country, so we always know about each other from community leaders and ... friends ... What happens to any Jain families ... their children ... and grandchildren ... the older generation ... we send out a search party to help and console them..."*

JINEN: (His lips quivering with agony in silence, mumbling...) *"My parents died together ... in the car crash, which blew up in flames..."*

CHANDRAMOHAN: *"My son, be brave ... every soul is the cause of its own happiness and misery. You are part of this unexplainable, unbearable loss ... Come, Let us pray to Lord Mahavirji for comfort..."*

Prayer.

NAVKAR MANTRA

Namo Arihantanam: I bow down to Arihanta,
Namo Siddhanam: I bow down to Siddha,
Namo Ayariyanam: I bow down to Acharya,
Namo Uvajjhayanam: I bow down to Upadhyaya,
Namo Loe Savva-sahunam: I bow down to Sadhu and Sadhvi.
Eso Panch Namokaro: These five bowing downs,

Savva-pavappanasano: Destroy all the sins,
Manglananch Savvesim: Amongst all that is auspicious,
Padhamam Havei Mangalam: This Navkar Mantra is the foremost.

The Navkar Mantra is the most important mantra in Jainism and can be recited at any time. While reciting the Navkar Mantra, we are bowing down with respect to Arihantas (souls who have reached the state of non-attachment towards worldly process), Siddhas (liberated souls), Ächäryäs (heads of sadhus and sadhvis), Upädhyäyas (those who teach scriptures to sadhus and sadhvis), Sädhus (monks, who have voluntarily given up social, economical and family relationships) and Sädhvis (nuns, who have voluntarily given up social, economical and family relationships). Collectively, they are called Panch Parmesthi (five supreme spiritual people). In this mantra we worship their virtues rather than worshipping any one particular person; therefore, this Mantra is not named after Lord Mahavir, Lord Parshvanath or Adinath, etc. When we recite Navkar Mantra, it also reminds us that, we need to be like them. This mantra is also called Namaskär or Namokär Mantra because we are bowing down.

The Navkär Mantra contains the main message of Jainism. The message is very clear. If we want to be liberated from this world then we have to take the first step of renunciation by becoming a monk or a nun. This is the beginning. If we stay on the right path then we will proceed to a higher state, Arihant, and ultimately proceed to Siddha after nirvana (liberation from the cycle of birth and death). The goal of every Jain is, or should be, to become a Siddha.

JINEN: (Helplessly shaking his head in sorrow)*"Comfort? Do I really need consultation? I need to cast off this burden of sorrow ... First Zarina and now my parents ... Is this all part of my karma..."*

CHANDRAMOHAN: *"Yes, yes ... my son ...all these bad deed are part of our karma..."*

JINEN: (In a demanding voice) *"What is karma, Guruji? What is all this bad karma that I have inherited?"*

CHANDRAMOHAN: (Talks about karma ... in short sentences...) *"In Jain theory, Karma is based on simple laws of cause and effect ... No effect is without a cause."*

JINEN: *"So everyone has to bear the consequences of their actions..."*

CHANDRAMOHAN: *"... And it is impossible to escape from Karma. It shows that human beings are the preserver or dispenser of justice. It inspires them to get their souls free of the karmic forces by developing will power and proper actions..."*

JINEN: *"What proper actions? I learned that karma can be burnt out by following physical and spiritual rituals and by giving up certain foods ... fasting - complete or partial? ..."*

CHANDRAMOHAN: *"Also, sitting on a rock in the hot sun or extreme cold and meditating. I had to pull out the hair by the roots, instead of shaving the head, to control the senses and emotions, asking for repentance for our sins..."*

JINEN: *"I need to ask for mercy ... I need to do repentance for my sins..."*

CHANDRAMOHAN: *"Sins?"*

JINEN: *"Yes, my sins, I am paying for my sins by loosing Zarina and my parents? I need your help..."*

CHANDRAMOHAN: *"Paying for your sins?"*

JINEN: *"Yes, Teach me to accept my life ... without Zarina and my parents. What is life all about ... we are born today ... living and dying ... gone tomorrow?"*

CHANDRAMOHAN: *"You are a lucky man ... Do you realize you are awakened by the gods to be a spiritual teacher ... most people ask these question when they are old and aging ... thinking of their passage between life and death. Don't forget this has been happening since the lifetime of our 24 Tirthankars (Jain God). These wise men found the answers to all these questions as they lived their daily lives as the householders and then taking the life of monks. All 24 attained moksha and became Siddhas..."*

JINEN: *"As a young man, my father taught me that every man is the architect of his own life..."*

CHANDRAMOHAN: *"True ... true but at the same time any man can aspire to attain perfection, irrespective of his religion, creed or caste..."*

JINEN: *"Where can I find this kind of peace? Do I have to fly all the way to India?"*

CHANDRAMOHAN: *"No. No, my son, you can start finding peace here in Siddhi Challum - Each day we preach ... a two fold training - first, for the layman* (Sravak) *and secondly for* *those interested in monkshood* (Priest Life) ... *making it possible for the spiritually weak to attain the level of a monk through slow and easy step by step ... you will never be alone..."*

JINEN: *"That is a comforting thought with everyone I love, gone ... forever..."*

CHANDRAMOHAN: *"Jinen, do not feel so rejected ... Here you will never be alone ... you will be serving the community daily..."*

JINEN: *"Guruji, first I want to change my life ... I want to start by doing pure seva* (rituals)..."

CHANDRAMOHAN: *"Jinen, then spend some time here at Siddhi Challum and think out your thoughts..."*

JINEN: *"I will need your help and guidance..."*

CHANDRAMOHAN: *"Son, I am always available to young people like you..."*

JINEN: *"For some reason, I need to try and start a new course of life for myself ... as I am filled with emptiness... I have no one left..."*

CHANDRAMOHAN: *"Walk with me into the temple and pray with me..."*

BOTH MEN ENTER THE TEMPLE ... They do the rituals of prayer ... and then exit...

Jinen tries to memorize all, closing his eyes.

ORIGINS OF JAINISM:

Originating on the Indian subcontinent, *Jainism* -- or, more properly, the Jain Religion (Dharma) -- is one of the oldest religions of its homeland and indeed of the world. Jainism has prehistoric origins dating before 3000 BC, and before the beginning of Indo-Aryanculture. Jain religion is unique in that, during its existence of over 5000 years, it has never compromised on the concept of nonviolence either in principle or practice. Jainism upholds nonviolence as the

Supreme religion (Ahimsa Paramo Dharmah) and has insisted upon its observance thought, word, and deed at the individual as well as social levels. The holy text Tattvartha Sutra sums it up in the phrase 'Parasparopagraho Jivanam' (all life is mutually supportive). Jain religion presents a truly enlightened perspective of equality of souls, irrespective of differing physical forms, ranging from human beings to animals and microscopic living organisms. Humans, alone among living beings, are endowed with all the six senses of seeing, hearing, tasting smelling, touching, and thinking; thus humans are expected to act responsibly towards all life by being compassionate, egoless, fearless, Forgiving, and rational.

THE JAIN CODE OF CONDUCT:

In short, the code of conduct is made up of the following five vows, and all of their logical conclusions: Ahimsa, Satya (truthfulness), Asteya (non-stealing), Aparigraha (non-possessiveness), and Brahmacharya (chastity). Jain religion focuses much attention on Aparigraha, non-possessiveness towards material things through self-control, self-imposed penance, abstinence from over-indulgence, voluntary curtailment of one's needs, and the consequent subsiding of the aggressive urge.

Jainism Beliefs and Practices

The universe exists as a series of layers, both heavens and hells. It had no beginning and will have no ending.

It consists of:

The supreme abode: This is located at the top of the universe and is where Siddha, the liberated souls, live.

The upper world: 30 heavens where celestial beings live.

Middle world: The earth and the rest of the universe.

Nether world: 7 hells with various levels of misery and punishments

The Nigoda or base: where the lowest forms of life reside

Universe space: Layers of clouds, which surround the upper world

Space beyond: An infinite volume without soul, matter, times, medium of motion or medium of rest. Everyone is bound within the universe by one's karma (the accumulated good and evil that one has done).

Moksha: (liberation from an endless succession of lives through reincarnation) is achieved by enlightenment, which can be attained only through asceticism. They are expected to follow five principles of living:

Ahimsa: Non violence in all parts of a person -- mental, verbal and physical. 3 Committing an act of violence against a human, animal, or even vegetable generates negative karma which in turn adversely affects one's next life.

Satya: Speaking truth; avoiding falsehood

Asteya: To not steal from others

Brahma-charya: (soul conduct) remaining sexually monogamous to one's spouse only

Aparigraha: Detach from people, places, and material things. Avoiding the collection of excessive material possessions, abstaining from over-indulgence, restricting one's needs, etc.

They follow Jains follow a vegetarian diet. (At least one information source incorrectly states that they follow a frutarian diet, the practice of only eating that which will not kill the plant or animal from which it is taken. e.g. milk, fruit, nuts.) They read their sacred texts daily. Jains are recommended to pass through four stages during their lifetime:

Brahmacharya-ashrama: The life of A student

Gruhasth-ashrama: Family life

Vanaprasth-ashrama: Family and social services

Sanyast-ashrama: Life as a monk a period of renunciation

Prayer of - Jain religion:

Every day Jain's bow their heads and say their universal prayer, the Navkar-mantra. All good work and events start with this prayer of salutation and worship.

Namaskar Mantra

- **Namo Arihantanam:** - I bow to the arithantas – the ever-perfect spiritual victors
- **Namo Siddhanam:** - I bow to the Siddhas the liberated souls
- **Namo Ayariyanam:** - I bow to acharyas – the leaders of the Jain order
- **Namo Uvajjayanam:** - I bow to upadhyayas the learned preceptors
- **Namo Loe Savva Sahunam:** - I bow to all saints and sages everywhere in the world
- **Eso Panch Namukkaro:** - These five obeisance's
- **Savva PavapPanasano:** - Erase all Sins
- **Mangalancha Savvesin:** - Amongst all that is auspicious
- **Padhamam Havai Mangalam:** - This is the foremost

In the above prayer, Jains do not ask for any favors or material benefits from their Gods, the Tirthankaras (Jain God) or from monks and nuns. They do not pray to a specific Tirthankara or monk by name. By saluting them, Jains receive the inspiration from the five benevolent for the right path of true happiness and total freedom from the misery of life

VEGETARIANISM

Vegetarianism is a way of life for a Jain, taking its origin in the Concept of compassion for living beings, Jiva Daya. The practice of vegetarianism is seen as an instrument for the practice of Nonviolence and peaceful, cooperative coexistence. Jains are strict vegetarians, consuming only one-sensed beings, primarily From the plant kingdom. While the Jain diet does, of course, involve harm to plants, it is regarded as a means of survival which involves The bare minimum amount of violence towards living beings. (Many forms of plant material, including roots and certain fruits, are also excluded from the Jain diet due to the greater number of living beings they contain owing to the environment in which they develop.).

Vegetarianism

As people become more conscious of their health problems, they are looking for newer, less pharmaceutical means of preserving and maintaining their health. A vegetarian diet which contains foods such as grains, beans, nuts, vegetables and fruit, is an important means to maintain one's health. Vegetarians, people whose diet does not include any meat products, eggs, poultry, or fish, are living proofs of the fact that vegetarian diet is healthier than non-vegetarian diet. Further, scientific research shows that meat is not essential for healthy living. So many people are switching to vegetarianism.

Everyone knows that proteins are necessary for good health. Proteins are needed daily to grow and repair tissues to maintain bodily functions. However, many people think that vegetarian diet is protein deficient. It may make people weak, sick, and anemic. They do not know that there is a multitude of vegetable protein sources. The National Research Council recommended that the average male should consume nine percent of calories in the form of protein. It should be noted that nine percent are more than double the minimum requirements established by the World Health Organization.

(1) Inspection of published food tables reveals that grains, legumes, nuts, seeds, and vegetables provide more than nine-percent calories in the form of proteins. Although vegetarians eat less protein than do meat eaters, they readily get as much as they need from non-flesh sources. Even vegans, who eat only plant foods, get more protein than the recommended level. This is true in view of the fact that non-vegetarian diet contains more non-essential proteins than vegetarian diet. Some people have the wrong belief that a lot of protein in diet can make them strong so they can do hard work. However, sports record show that vegetarian athletes surpass or at least do as well as other athletes in events that require strength and endurance, such as running, swimming, and tennis. For instance, Pierreo Verot, a vegetarian, holds the world record for downhill endurance skiing. The world record for distance butterfly swimming is held by vegetarians James and Jonathan deDonato.

(2) Furthermore, vegetarians are more readily able to attain physical balance, mental clarity, and spiritual harmony? Factors that are critical in maintaining optimal health Formerly, vegetable proteins were classified as second-class, and regarded as inferior to first-class proteins of animal origin, but this distinction has now been generally discarded.

(3) Now it has been found that excessive amount of protein found in meat products is not only nonessential but it is actually hazardous to our health. For example, osteoporosis and kidney stones have been linked to over-consumption of proteins. Researchers at University of Michigan and other universities have shown that the more protein a person consumes, the more calcium his or her body loses, resulting in osteoporosis. The high-protein (meat-based) diets result in gradual decrease in bone density and cause osteoporosis. The results of the study indicate that vegetarian men have an average bone loss of three percent while non-vegetarian men, seven percent. Vegetarian women have an average bone loss of eighteen percent and non-vegetarian women, thirty-five percent. The study also shows that by the time a non-vegetarian woman reaches the age of sixty-five, she has lost over one-third of her skeletal structure. On the contrary, vegetarian women tend to remain active, maintain their skeletal structure, and are less likely to fracture or break their bones.

(4) Another problem caused by excessive protein is the formation of kidney stones. Kidney stones are caused by crystallization of calcium that is lost from the bones in digesting excessive amounts of protein. There is some evidence that excessive protein consumption can result in destruction of kidney tissue and the deterioration of kidneys. This is because kidneys have to work harder to de-aminize and excrete the excess protein out of the body.

(5) Besides proteins, saturated fats, such as animal fats, and cholesterol play an important role in a person's health. Although some fats are necessary in a balanced diet for body maintenance, saturated fats can be hazardous to one's health if they are taken in excess amounts. Animal fats are heavier and stickier than vegetable fats. The heavier the fat, the more it agglutinates blood cells, thus increasing the viscosity of blood, restricting blood flow and raising blood pressure. If the blood stops moving freely, it can cause a clot in the artery. These clots can lead to heart disease. Similarly, cholesterol, which is found in large amounts in non-vegetarian food, deposits in artery walls and causes the arteries to clog, resulting in angina and other problems. 'Although absent in plant foods, cholesterol is present in meat, poultry, seafood, dairy products, and eggs. Cholesterol is the main component of the plaque that builds up in arteries, causing atherosclerosis (disease of arteries).' All of these foods, with the exception of seafood, are also high in saturated fat. Diets high in saturated fats and cholesterol increase cholesterol level in blood and produce atherosclerosis, which leads to heart disease and stroke. Diets low in saturated fat and cholesterol keep cholesterol level low and thus lower the probability of heart disease and stroke. Nutritional studies show that vegetarians consume less cholesterol and saturated fats and have lower levels of cholesterol. Studies also show that meat eaters have higher rates of atherosclerosis and fatal heart disease. In a study, the risk of fatal coronary heart disease among the non-vegetarian members of a group was found to be three tines greater than that for the vegetarian members of the group.

(6) Thus AHA advises avoiding foods that have a lot of saturated fat and cholesterol, which are found mainly in animal products and recommends that people should use beans, lentils, tofu, and other plant foods instead of meat in their meals. A vegetarian diet with lower saturated fat content helps to reverse heart disease. Dr. Dean Ornish has been prescribing vegetarian diet to people with heart disease. It is found that a significantly low fat content in diet is the key ingredient in restoring health. Dr. Ornish, the head of heart disease reversal studies, says, 'If everyone in the country was eating a low fat vegetarian diet, heart disease could be as rare as malaria.' Recently, Harvard University and Michio Kushi completed a study to discern the effects of macrobiotic on blood and cardiovascular strength and overall condition. People who normally maintained vegetarian diet were asked to change to a more standard American diet, containing meat, heavy sauces, sweets, and processed foods. After a few weeks, the results showed that their cardiovascular systems were affected adversely by the American diet.

(7) In addition to heart disease, colon and breast cancers are also linked to consumption of excessive saturated fat and cholesterol. The Association for the Advancement of Science states that 'populations on high meat, high fat diet are more likely to develop colon cancer than people on vegetarian diet.'

(8) Evidence from a study conducted in Stockholm, Sweden, reports that the greater the fat intake of a person, the higher the risk he or she has of contracting colon cancer. Similarly, the more fat a woman consumes in her lifetime, the more likely she is to get breast cancer. In a study conducted at the National Cancer Research Institute in Tokyo by Dr. Hirayama and his coworkers, the results show that women who consume meat daily face an almost four times greater risk of getting breast cancer than those who eat no meat.

(9) Avoiding meats and substituting plant proteins can have amazing effects on general health and well being. Not only that, but a vegetarian diet can, in many cases, actually reverses diseases. Many miraculous cancer remissions effected by adopting a vegetarian diet have been reported. One instance is the case of Dr. Anthony Sattilaro who was diagnosed with prostate cancer in 1978. He underwent traditional medical therapy but the cancer spread to his lungs. When he had only six months to live, he discovered the benefits of a vegetarian diet. Eighteen months after Dr. Satlilaro had switched to a vegetarian diet, a CAT scan performed on him showed that he was completely rid of both cancers.

(10) As mentioned above, some non-vegetarians believe that vegetarians are weak, skinny, and anemic. However, it is seen that most vegetarians' experience better than average health and typically live physically active and demanding lives. People who have adopted a vegetarian diet experience many benefits. They sleep better, though for fewer hours. But they wake up feeling more refreshed and energetic than they did before. Many new vegetarians feel 'they are now able to participate in life more than they thought possible.'

(11) In addition to these physical benefits, a vegetarian can enjoy his or her meals without guilt and without considering the meals to be a form of punishment. Vegetarian meals can be prepared in may different ways to suit different tastes. Some vegetarians feel that they can eat more foods with fewer calories, fat, and cholesterol. A vegetarian diet can have some shortcomings if it is not prepared properly. For example, some foods may have too much salt. They cause water to be drawn out of blood cells, creating dehydration of tissues and result in the problem of water retention in the body. Excessive sodium overburdens the kidneys and forces the heart to work twice as hard. This leads to hypertension? increased blood pressure. Another problem with a vegetarian diet is that some people may not consume dark green and leafy vegetables, which are a major source of essential vitamins A and E. A proper combination of grains, beans and vegetables is essential to develop an ideal amino acid pattern for the body. For example, combination of corn tortilla and beans, wheat bread and lentils, or beans and rice are good sources of protein. The foods that were once believed to be the foundation of good health in some parts of the world are actually detrimental to one's health and cause diseases like cancer, heart disease, osteoporosis, and kidney stones. On the other hand, those foods that were once looked upon by some people as nutritionally deficient have now been proven to be healthy and helpful in maintaining our health and reversing diseases. Now it has been established that a balanced vegetarian diet is the healthier choice for the well being of people all over the world.

There are two important reasons for adopting vegetarianism. Many people are vegetarians because of their religious beliefs. Others are vegetarians because a vegetarian diet is good for health. Jains are vegetarians because they believe in nonviolence. Violence means to kill or injure, to be angry or be greedy, to engage in self-torture, to be intolerant, not listening to what other people are saying, etc. If we do not take proper care of our body and mind, we are committing violence of self. A vegetarian diet is natural and better for our health as described below. Thus vegetarianism helps us avoid violence of self. Vegetarians do not eat meat, poultry, or fish. There are three kinds of vegetarians, based on their attitude to milk and eggs. Vegans do not take eggs or milk. Lactose's do not eat eggs but they do drink milk. Lacto-ovo's eat eggs and drink milk. Jains are lactose.

Here are some health reasons why some people don't eat meat:

1) To protect their heart. Animal fat and high cholesterol diet may set a stage for heart disease. In some places where very little fat is eaten, the death rate from heart disease is lower than in other places.

2) To reduce the risk of cancer. Animal fat and cholesterol have been linked to some forms of cancer such as the cancer of colon, breast, and uterus. The National Academy of Sciences reported in 1983 that 'people may be able to prevent many common cancers by eating less fatty meats and more vegetables and grains.' A vegetarian diet also reduces the risk of kidney trouble.

3) To control their weight. Vegetarian diet is bulky and filling. The caloric value of a six-ounce steak (with its fat) equals that of a whole pound of cooked noodles. Thus most people lose weight when they go on a vegetarian diet. This also reduces the risk of high blood pressure, diabetes, and back troubles.

Man is vegetarian by nature. Vegetarian food is more suited to the human body. We do not require animal proteins for strength and energy. A physiological comparison of meat-eater, herbivore, and man proves this statement. A meat-eater has claws, has no skin pores, and perspires through the tongue. A meat-eater has sharp front teeth for tearing and no flat molars for grinding. The intestinal tract of a meat eater is only three times his body length so that rapidly decaying meat can pass out quickly. A meat-eater has strong hydrochloric acid in stomach to digest meat. A herbivore has no claws and perspires through skin pores. He does not have sharp front teeth and has flat rear molars. His intestinal tract is about ten times the body length, and stomach acid, twenty times less strong than meat-eaters. A man has no claws, perspires through skin pores, has no sharp front teeth, and has flat rear molars. The intestinal tract of a man is twelve times his body length, and stomach acid, twenty times less strong than meat-eaters. Once within the stomach, meat requires digestive juices high in hydrochloric acid. A man's stomach does not have it. Another important fact is that our intestinal tract is too long where food is further digested and nutrients are passed into the blood. The putrefaction of meat in our long intestinal tract produces poisonous wastes. That is why meat must be eliminated from our diet.

The basic foods in a vegetarian diet are cereals, grains, bread, nuts, beans, seeds, fruits, and vegetables. Most vegetable proteins are incomplete and most animal proteins are complete. Our bodies require complete proteins to function properly. So vegetarians combine vegetable proteins in a way that makes them complete. Two or more vegetables and grains, nuts, etc., having incomplete proteins, can be combined in a meal to form complete proteins. Here are three simple ways to do it:

1. Combine legumes (dried peas, beans, lentils) with grains (barley, wheat, rice, rye). **2.** Combine legumes with nuts and seeds. **3.** Combine milk products with any vegetable protein.

If we practice vegetarianism, we will be able to satisfy our religious beliefs and also maintain our health

'At work and at parties, Americans are drinking less and enjoying it more ', is the subheading of the cover story of the Time Magazine of May 20, 1985. The article points towards the growing trend towards temperance in the U. S. A.

The author writes:
The temperate mood is transforming the ways, in which the nation works, plays, and socializes. New attitudes towards careers, fitness, and the very image of what we are and wish to become are being altered. Americans are tackling the entrenched social problems of abusive drinking with new rigor. The neo-temperance has already inspired tough drunk-driving laws to combat highway bloodshed. Basic to it all: people are drinking lighter. Only 67% of the nation's 170 million adults over 18 said that they drink at all.' We Jains can easily remain with the 33% who don't drink at all.

The writer has further remarked:
For the fitness-conscious, alcohol has joined sodium and cholesterol as a substance devoutly to be avoided. The active ingredient in alcohol is ethanol, a depressant closely akin to ether. It dulls perception, slows reaction, and contains 'empty' carbohydrate calories, that is, with no nutritional value.

Jainism says that the dulling of perception and slowing of reaction is violence toward the self because it is, in fact, partially obstructing one's life processes unnecessarily. It can also lead to other kinds of violence. Therefore consumption of alcohol and of other such drugs is prohibited in Jainism.

Some people may say that alcohol relieves stress by releasing endorphins, chemicals that calm the nervous system. However, studies have shown that endorphins are released by physical exercise just as well. Righteous meditation can also cause the release of endorphins. Thus it is not necessary to take alcohol for the purpose of relieving tension. Moreover, in the case of alcohol and other habit-forming drugs, there is the potential risk of going overboard. Alcohol is the most widely abused drug.

Rationalism entails that we do not succumb to peer pressure and that we avoid situations that may lead to ill-health dependence on unnecessary substances, conflicts, and violence. Thus we should stay away from alcohol and drugs.

WHAT IS SECT?

To Create a Class which accepts appropriate ethics-thoughts out of multiple Views-principles of religion considering the several views as main principle is called Sect.

WHAT IS SWETAMBER?

Wearing Swet (White) clothes lifetime and meditate to achieve an ultimate goal is called Swetamber.

WHAT IS DIGAMBER?

Clothes hindrance to acquire the Kevalgnan and hence to become less clothed and to meditate to achieve the last goal is called Digamber.

Jina and the Soul

Jainism: The 'Jains' are the followers of the **Jinas**. **'Jina'** literally means

Conqueror: He who has conquered love and hate, pleasure and pain, attachment and aversion, and has thereby freed `his' soul from the karmas obscuring knowledge, perception, truth, and ability, is a Jina. The Jains refer to the Jina as God.

What is Tirthankara?
A tirthankara is one who establishes Jain organization after conquering both love and hatred. He shows a fine path to the living beings of the world to be free from ignorance, misery, and moha (Worldly happiness)

What do Tirthankaras do?
The 24 Tirthankaras are considered to be the creator of Jain religion. They are divine elements of Jainism. They have attained all the achievement of ultimate nature including the ultimate knowledge after making vigorous efforts. Their principles are for betterment and welfare of others. Their path is to provide total fearless life and that of non-violence and to distribute love and friendship. Their vision of life is very wide and they have no insistence for anything. Their way of life is for giving up possessive passion and being free from the karmas we have a brief introduction of all 24 Tirthankaras, who are generous, noble passion-free and very holy characters.

Why there are 24 Tirthankaras only?
The answer to this question can be perhaps available from the 87th stanza of "Yashstilakchulikc" scripture written by Acharya Somdev Suri. He observes:

'There are indefinite number of Grahas (Planets) – Nakshatras – Stars (Heavenly elements in the sky). But their numbers are shown to be limited by the rule of nature. In the present era of Utsarpini time-span, there are 24 times only when these heavenly elements are positioned in the best location. This is a certainty. Therefore there are only 24 Tirthankaras only not a one less not a one more.

Name of Tirthankars
Lord Rishabhdev: He had a sign of an ox on his thigh. The mother Marudeva had seen 14 dreams, of which the first was that of an ox. He started the religion after a time span of 18 Koda Kodi Sagaropam (Sagaropam itself is almost an innumerable number, therefore 18 KodaKodi sagaropam is a countless number) Therefore, he was known as Adinath also (The first one)

Lord Ajitnath: When mother Vijaya Rani and Father Jitshatru was playing chess; the queen was winning and winning. She did not lose. Likewise, the Lord did not lose. He won the enemies like love and hates.

Lord Sambhavnath: On his birth, there was plenty of crops everywhere. There was no famine, or draught. All these characteristics were of a good person. Therefore he was known as Sambhavnath.

Lord Abhinandan Swami: When he was conceived in mother's womb, Lord Indra made frequent visits and praised

Him. People in the family and the state became happy and they congratulated each other. So his name was decided

Lord Sumatinat: Once mother, while finding solution to a very difficult problem, got good intellect and she could resolve the conflict peacefully. So he was good 'Mati'. He was known as Sumatinat.

Lord Padmaprabh: The mother desired to sleep on lotus leaf. The lord also was as unattached as Lotus flower

Lord Suparshvanath: The mother had a disease on both the sides, but when the Lord Supashva was conceived, she was totally cured and became glittering like gold.

Lord Chandra Prabha Swami: Mother had a desire to drink the nectar from moon. She had a feeling of coolness.

Lord Suvidhinath: When He was in mother's womb, he had desired to perform good deeds. He became one performing good deeds.

Lord Shitalnath: The father had a very strong burning fever, which could be calmed down by a cool touch of his mother. He also cooled down threefold burning of the world.

Lord Shreyanshnath: There was a bed, set out by some God. It was worshipped, but could not be taken in use. The mother used in but nothing happened due to the great Lord's grace, who was in the womb. On the contrary the world became happier

Lord Vasupujya: Indra made Frequent showers of diamonds / Wealth. He got the name Vasupujya from the name of His father Vasudev

Lord Vimalnath: When He was in mother's womb, both the body and the mind became pure with his grace. The Lord destroyed the unclean karmas with purity of this mind.

Lord Anantnath: The mother had a dream of a garland made from numerous precious giens likewise, with a thread within innumerable knots, the fever and other illness of people disappeared. The Lord performed worship for indefinite period, for three fold jwelves

Lord Dharmanath: The mother became more prone to religion. The lord himself was by nature prone to religion

Lord Shantinath: When he was in mother's womb, all the disease and misdeeds disappeared. There was peace all around

Lord Kunthunath: In a dream, a big pillar made from Jewelry was seen. The enemies became as small as the Lord took care of 'Kunthu' Besides small tiny creatures

Lord Arnath: In the dream was seen the wheel with jewel and the pillar. This resulted in growth of the dynasty
Lord Mallinath: The mother had a desire to sleep in a bed decorated with flowers of all the six seasons. This desire was fulfilled by Gods. The lord won the Moha etc.

Lord Munisuvrat Swami: Mother had a desire to keep best vows; and she kept 12 such vows.

Lord Naminath: When the mother was moving on the fort, her luster could not be seen and faced by the enemies. They bowed down. The lord also got the love and hatred bowed down to him.

Lord Neminath: (Lord Aristhnemi) **Aristha** means black jewel. Mother saw such black jewel saw a shining wheel. The lord is also as good as sharp edge of the Religious wheel to destroy the Karmas

Lord Parshvanath: Mother saw a snake passing by a bed of the king without doing any injury (biting) to the king.

Lord Mahavir SwamiLord Vardhman: There was a constant increase in wealth, crops, prosperity, achievements etc., parents grew with more and more fame. The Lord became fearless, firm, and brave.

JINEN: (Sighs, opening his eyes and looking at the garden) *"I feel such peace here ... as if I have come home..."*

CHANDRAMOHAN: *"I am glad, this is a good feeling after the loss of your parents and Zarina. You have really gone through a great deal of misfortune these last few days..."*

JINEN: *"May be, I should stay here for a while ... May be, I should think of becoming a monk..."*

CHANDRAMOHAN: *"Please do not make ... or take ... such a serious decision in a hurry ... You have your whole life ahead of you..."*

JINEN: *"Tell me Guruji, Is it true that the life of a ascetic ... you know, Jain monk ... is most austere and rigorous --*

compared with any other religion in the world, especially the principles observed by monks who desire to free themselves from rebirths ... to attain Moksha?"

CHANDRAMOHAN: *"Moksha, my son, is complete deliverance consequent on the dissolution of Karma ... to achieve Moksha ... means ... ultimate salvation with no possibility of rebirths ... or ... reincarnation..."*

JINEN: *"... Ultimate salvation with no more rebirths? Nirvana?"*

CHANDRAMOHAN: *"Consider your last time here ... you spoke of your beloved wife Zarina ... You were able to feel her spiritual presence in these beautiful gardens?"*

JINEN: *"Yes... I have been thinking long and hard ...We had this wonderful conversation under the moonlight."*

CHANDRAMOHAN: *"You are speaking of Zarina?"*

JINEN: *"Yes, she will always live in my heart."*

CHANDRAMOHAN: *"Yes, her spirit will always be with you..."*

JINEN: *"Guruji, I feel I am ready to face the world..."*

CHANDRAMOHAN: *"Nothing will come easy Jinen ... to become a Jain monk you will have to relinquish everything ... give up all feelings of passion, desires, dreams and your destiny ... ambition ... pride..."*

JINEN: *"I can do that ... I am prepared to give up everything for once ... a peace of mind..."*

CHANDRAMOHAN: *"As you are still very young, you will face many temptations..."*

JINEN: *"I am not afraid to face my own demons. Can you teach me to free myself of passion, anger, love and hate?"*

CHANDRAMOHAN: *"Yes. You will need more time to make this major decision in your life..."*

JINEN: *"For this I will need your blessings..."*

CHANDRAMOHAN: *"Jinen, define desire?"*

JINEN: *"Desire simply desires things ... love ... ambition..."*

CHANDRAMOHAN: *"No, my son, desire is an expression of one's own incompleteness..."*

JINEN: (Repeats the words of the monk as though he is digesting the thought) *"Desire is an expression of one's own incompleteness?"*

CHANDRAMOHAN: *"Tell me, what do you want to achieve by becoming a monk?"*

JINEN: *"At this stage in my life, I consider life a precious commodity and I want to spend it wisely and doing seva..."*

CHANDRAMOHAN: *"Taking the path of monkshood is a difficult journey of sacrifice... begging for your food..."*

JINEN: *"You have already mentioned it..."*

CHANDRAMOHAN: *"Do you know what Apargrah means?"*

JINEN: *"I learned all that since I was a child..."*

CHANDRAMOHAN: *"You will have to devote your whole life in the path of Ahimsa - Non Violence... never seeking any revenge from your enemies till the day you die"*

JINEN: *"I need to conquer all my desires..."*

CHANDRAMOHAN: *"Have you endured intense physical pain unable to bear?"*

JINEN: *"No physical and mental pain can compare with what I have endured with the loss of my Zarina and my parents..."*

CHANDRAMOHAN: *"To become a monk ...you have to pluck your hair ...etc."*

JINEN: *"Guruji, my mind is made up ... help me to get the strength to endure the suffering..."*

CHANDRAMOHAN: *"There is a great deal of reading books, the shastras* {old religions books} *the scriptures and philosophy and start to live in accordance to the ancient customs and traditions...'*

JINEN: *"Pray for my success"*

CHANDRAMOHAN: *"I will try to be here whenever you need me"*

JINEN: *"Then I am ready to start as soon as possible"*

CHANDRAMOHAN: *"Any last minute thoughts?"*

JINEN: *"Guruji, Not at this time. I will need to settle things in the outside world ... Once again I thank you...'*

CHANDRAMOHAN: *"Before you leave ... please do not forget to contact Dr. Gandhi or if you want, I will phone him myself to tell him you are in good hands."*

JINEN: *"I will phone him ... He is always worrying ... Yes, and I must tell him about this ... my decision..."*

Young man Jinen is seen walking against the landscape of Siddhi Challum. He is staring into the blue sky, breathing in the clean fresh air smiling to himself as if he is suddenly at peace with himself not a worried expression on his face just a glowing smile. His eyes calm and penetrating.

The theme song will be played as an echoing rhythm bringing in a melancholy atmosphere, nostalgia as the audience start to recognize the theme song associated with his love for Zarina.

Theme Song.

Whose love? This is all I think.
Our love is in the village of the heart.
He will not see me stopping here ever.
To watch our true love fill up with happiness.
Our little horse love may think it queer.
To stop without a secret love farmhouse near.
Between two lovers will be the "STORM" of the century.
He gives harness bells shake.
To ask if there is some error.
The only other skies that sweep.
Of stormy wind and downy flake.
The two lovers are great, sparkling soul.
But I have committed to keep.
And miles to fly in ending love.
Before I sleep...
Before I sleep...

FLASH BACK

Part 13

Scenes: Hospital where Jinen is seen knocking on Dr. Gandhi's office door.

DR. GANDHI: *"The door is open ... come in."*

JINEN: (Opens the door and enters ... finding Dr. Gandhi looking at an old x-ray report) *"Hey Dr. Uncle ... Do you want to see me."*

DR. GANDHI: *"Oh, Hello ... Jinen ... Come, come, sit down, sit down"* (Pointing to the chair ... Jinen sits in front of him, looking at him in earnest)

JINEN: (Fear in his eyes ...as he bite his lip) *"Dr. Uncle, how are my parents? I need to see them..."*

DR. GANDHI: (Closes the x-ray report ...looks at Jinen ... hesitatingly) *"Jinen ... Yes ... I am glad you came ... I did not want to break the news on the phone* (Pause) *but tell you myself..."*

JINEN: *"What is it Rajiv Uncle, break what news to me?"*

DR. GANDHI: *"Well, son, you heard ... your parents had a car accident"*

JINEN: *"No ... Are they all right? When? How ... Where did it happen? Can I see..."*

DR. GANDHI: *"No ... You have to be very brave ... they did not survive the car crash..."*

JINEN: (He stands and stares at Dr. Gandhi in disbelief) *"What are you saying ... Oh, my god, my god ... Uncle ... Dr. Uncle.... Please, can I see them ... please don't tell me..."*

DR. GANDHI: *"I...I am sorry to tell you this terrible news ... but they are no more ... both your mother and father ...I am sorry"*

JINEN: (Slamming the chair, screaming) *"No more ... No more ... what are you saying, my God ... No more..."*

DR. GANDHI: (Rushes to his side ... trying to control him) *"Jinen, please try and control yourself ... This is not easy for me to say ... I can imagine what you are going through..."*

JINEN: *"What is happening, first Zarina and now my parents?"*

DR. GANDHI: *"Yes ... this is a great loss..."*

JINEN: (He is weeping uncontrollable, his whole body quivering and shaking with guilt) *"Why is ... this happening to me? Oh. Lord Mahavirji, what have I done to deserve this curse ... this terrible karma ... Why am I being punished ... for what?"*

DR. GANDHI: *"Go ahead and weep ... it will lighten the burden in your heart ... You know how close I was to your* *father ... to your family ... We were so close, helping each other through the years..."*

JINEN: (He looks up, his face is tearless though his body is throbbing painfully) *"Doctor, I don't have any more tears left ... but I can feel throbbing pain in my heart ... What ... How did it happen? When?"*

DR. GANDHI: *"They came to visit you at the hospital -- but you had gone ... So your mother felt sure you had returned home. She frantically suggested to your father to take her home immediately ... She was sure you had gone home."*

JINEN: *"No ... No ... I drove to Siddhi Challum..."*

DR. GANDHI: (Pause) *"well, fifteen/twenty minutes later, I got this phone call from the police station reporting a terrible accident on the highway.... Your father must have been driving very fast in the traffic. I was told the car skidded off the road, over the bridge and crashed into a gasoline truck which caught on fire ... When I reached the scene of the accident ... there were three or four ambulances ... and they brought back two bodies ... burned beyond recognition ...to the hospital.... Police were everywhere and the traffic came to a standstill for over 2-3 hours..."*

JINEN: (Stunned ... his eyes gazing out of the window...) *"Car, caught on fire ... burned to death ... both Mom and Dad?"*

DR. GANDHI: *"Jinen, please know ... they did not suffer ... It was all a matter of minutes ... seconds ... the crash, the fire explosion."*

JINEN: *"Fire explosion ... what a horrible way to die ... my dear Mom and Dad ... my soul weeps for you..."*

DR. GANDHI: *"The moment of death comes completely unexpected..."*

JINEN: *"Why all this suffering with Zarina's death? I exhausted my life following her spirit everywhere as though we were inseparable in death. Lord Mahavirji (Jain God), have mercy on me ... why all this darkness? ... My body suffers and my soul weeps ... that I have been left alive ... I feel so miserable…"*

DR. GANDHI: *"We are bitter victims with this sudden separation ... this passing away of your parents ... Your father was my greatest friend..."*

JINEN: *"Why am I surrounded with so much dying and death ... Is there a lesson here I have to learn?"*

DR. GANDHI: *"I wish I had an answer for you ... As a doctor, I have learned early that we have no control over life and death..."*

JINEN: *"But none of them deserved to die ... for what? I no longer believe in the existence of God? He is only a myth, nothing else..."*

DR. GANDHI: *"Jinen, this has nothing to do with God..."*

JINEN: *"Then what is the real reason for living and dying?"*

DR. GANDHI: *"You are very confused and there is no way you can think rationally ... Please let me help you ... Come and* *stay with me and my family for a few days, so that this will all pass..."*

JINEN: *"It seems like the whole world is falling apart ... my very own soul is torn away from my body ... I cannot burden you and your family with my problems. Please forgive me ... I need to be alone..."*

DR. GANDHI: *"At least come home tonight ... you can have a room all to yourself ... We have to complete the arrangements for the funeral."*

JINEN: *"Yes, yes ... I seemed to have forgotten."*

DR. GANDHI: *"My wife has been making the funeral arrangements and we request your presence to perform the final cremation rituals ... Your parents would have want that..."*

JINEN: *"Yes, yes..."*

The song of goodbye is played as we see flames rising up to the sky superimposed with people departing. Then Jinen appears full face dressed in white kurta pajamas.

Goodbye Song.

Listen my friends
Life is short, but beautiful
Coming in this earth as a creature
When? Where we will finish our journey?
We believe everything is in Gods hands
Why do you cry for this death?
Everybody comes alone and leaves alone
That's the law of God

Oh Dear Friends, Last goodbye to your loved ones
Smile with tears and pray
Complete your duties
Life Goes on

DR. GANDHI: (His hand on Jinen's shoulder) *"Your parents will be very proud of the ceremony ... You performed the rituals to perfection..."*

JINEN: *"It was a traumatic experience..."*

DR. GANDHI: *"It was a very traditional Jain ritual and the Guruji taught you well..."*

KEVIN: (Greets Jinen, laying his hand on his shoulders) *"Well, that was an awesome ceremony ... You looked like a priest ... mastering each ritual with such confidence"*

JINEN: *"Yes, it was a beautiful farewell to my parents ... I had no idea what I was doing ... even though Guruji explained every word and action..."*

DR. GANDHI: *"So, you are welcome to remain in our home for as long as you like..."*

JINEN: *"Thank you so much ... you have been a true friend of my father's ... I can't think what I could have done without you ... these few days..."*

DR. GANDHI: *"Jinen, you always have a family with us ... my home will always be yours ... consider us as your family now..."*

JINEN: *"Thank you ... I will remember - but I am being drawn to the solitude at Siddhi Challum (Temple) ... and I would like to spend some time there ... if you will permit me."*

KEVIN: *"Yea, it is the perfect place for solitude and meditation ... But listen to your doctor, you need people around you ... during this stage of sorrow..."*

JINEN: *"For some unknown reason, I am drawn to that place ... I feel at peace ... content."*

KEVIN: *"You can always stay at my place..."*

JINEN: *"And share the miserable me? ... Never..."*

KEVIN: *"I thought we were friends, Man."*

JINEN: *"Friendship will always be there ... You saved my life ... you are more than a brother to me ... but I have something more important to find out..."*

KEVIN: *"Well, brother ... you always have a room at my place, remember that..."*

JINEN: *"That is nice to know, as we still have to find out who killed Zarina. All the police questioning us have bought no suspects. But they are still on the case. So let's keep in touch ... though I have decided to spend time in Siddhi Challum..."*

KEVIN: *"Dr. Gandhi please put some sense into Jinen ... He needs to be with family and friends..."*

DR. GANDHI: *"Jinen, I think Kevin is right..."*

JINEN: *"Please try and understand ... I needed to get away from New York City ... and I have found a rare kind of peace..."*

DR. GANDHI: *"Okay, then promise you will keep in touch with us and not try anything out of the ordinary..."*

JINEN: *"That period of my life is over ... especially as I started to do yoga and meditate ... I no longer feel suicidal."*

Part 14

A tall handsome man, Mustak is walking towards the mall, he is Zarina's fathers best friend's son. She sees him and waves, joining him carrying two ice cream cones handing him one while she start having the other...

MUSTAK: (He teases her, happy to see her) *"Zarina ... this is great ... what are you doing at the mall..."*

ZARINA: *"Mustak, how are you ... have not seen you for some time at the prayers on Fridays?"*

MUSTAK: *"I have been so busy with my real estate exams. Anyway, I don't hang around at malls ... But it is so nice to see you..."*

ZARINA: *"Ah, ha ... there are some very nice girls here ... I am sure you will be interested ... I had to come here to do some shopping with Mom..."*

MUSTAK: *"Glad to know you are not alone ... I guess you ladies have to do your shopping..."*

ZARINA: *"Oh, the whole family is here ... everyone loves to walk around at the mall ... and visit the different shops ... but I have to leave..."*

MUSTAK: *"You see me and say, "I have to leave..." Why are you in a hurry?'*

ZARINA: *"I want to get home to my apartment in the city, before it gets late ... dark."*

MUSTAK: *"If you are traveling alone, I should accompany you ... I am sure your father will not mind..."*

ZARINA: *"Father will never mind ... you are his favorite..."*

MUSTAK: *"Am I also your favorite?"*

ZARINA: *"Favorite? "*

MUSTAK: *"It is important for me to see your father today ... can I come along with you before you leave for the city?"*

ZARINA: *"Well, Mom has the car ... and I was going to grab a taxi ... so if you have your car, then may be I can take a ride home?"*

MUSTAK: *"Okay, let's go..."*

ZARINA: *"What is it that you want to talk to my Dad about? I can give him the message..."*

MUSTAK: *"No, no ... I need to pay my respect and discuss something important..."*

ZARINA: *"As you wish..."*

MUSTAK: *"Aren't you interested in knowing what I want to discuss with your father?"*

ZARINA: *"I am sure it is something you men like discussing ... maybe a job in his real estate company?"*

MUSTAK: *"No, it is more important than that ... He has always told me that once I pass my exams, I have a job..."*

ZARINA: *"I don't really care..."*

MUSTAK:*"You really should care, baby..."*

ZARINA: *"Mustak, you're kidding ... aren't you ... What are you talking about?"*

MUSTAK: (Laughs with ironic facial expression ... taunting her) *"I thought I should mention that you have a new Desi boyfriend"*

ZARINA *"Are you mad? No, you must be crazy..."*

MUSTAK: *"Am I? I have seen you with him several times in town ... Its time your parents know who you are meeting."*

ZARINA: *"But it is none of your business ... Or do you want me to bribe you..."*

MUSTAK: *"Yes, it is everyone's business as I am your friend. And I adore you..."*

ZARINA: *"No you don't..."*

MUSTAK: *"Our fathers have discussed that we both should marry..."*

ZARINA: *"Stop kidding ... You are joking aren't you?"*

MUSTAK: *"I have never been more serious."*

ZARINA: *"It can never be ... you know your problem..."*

MUSTAK: *"You are my problem..."*

ZARINA: *"Well, I have seen you snorting white powder and injecting crack at parties and even at home..."*

MUSTAK: *"No, you were imagining it ... I have never taken that stuff ... I swear I am clean..."*

ZARINA: *"Yea, look at yourself ... your eyes are blood shot red ... you have had something ... I can tell..."*

MUSTAK: *"But I can still talk with your father."*

ZARINA: *"You know that my father knows you take drugs ... what's this vendetta? ...Please leave me alone..."*

MUSTAK: *"You are part of the Christian family ... dating a complete desi stranger..."*

ZARINA: *"Mustak, please go away ... I suspected you came to the Mall deliberately to see me..."*

MUSTAK: *"Okay, don't make a scene ... I have just snorted a little ... I needed a pick up to talk with you.... I am done with you for now, but you better behave and not be seen around with those desi guys. I am warning you ... I will not tolerate it..."*

ZARINA: (She walks away from him without a word ... and hails a cab)

MUSTAK: *"Yea, go ahead ... walk away ... I will still talk to your father about us ... you can't stop me..".*

ZARINA: (Enters the cab and flips her cellphone dialing Jinen's number) *"Hello ... hey ... what are you doing?"*

JINEN: (Voice from her cellphone)*"Hi, the love of my life ... do you miss me?"*

ZARINA: (Her eyes filled with tears ... smiling) *"I need to see you ... I am nervous ... where are you?"*

JINEN: (VOICE from her cellphone) *"I miss you more ... Do you know we are getting married in 48 hours? Just stay calm for two more days ... and all our worries will be over..."*

ZARINA: *"But we haven't told my parents."*

JINEN: (Voice from her cellphone) *"We are both grown up ... after my parents behavior ... your parents may react the same way ... I told you we have to take our destiny into our own hands and say nothing to anyone ... If we don't do it my way ... we will never be married ... and you are the only woman in the world I want to spend the rest of my life with ... together..."*

ZARINA: *"Jinen, I feel so bad I am betraying my parent's trust me* **...** *and now we have another problem..."*

JINEN: (Voice from her cellphone) *"Problem..."*

ZARINA: *"Remember, I spoke to you about Mustak ... the one who is a druggie ... he wants to tell my father about us"*

JINEN: *"Oh, is that all ... You almost gave me a heart attack ... Your father will never permit you to marry a drug addict..."*

ZARINA: *"I am still worried ... you never know with Mustak..."*

JINEN: *"Who is Mustak?"*

ZARINA: *"You know I told you about him ... we practically grew up together ... He is the son of my father's best friend..."*

JINEN: *"Why don't you invite him to the wedding?"*

ZARINA: *"Jinen, don't joke ... He's seen me with you several times and he threatens to tell my father about us."*

JINEN: *"Does he know we are getting married? Did you tell him?"*

ZARINA: *"No ... what to do think I am ... some kind of an idiot? ... But he threatened to go and meet my parents and tell them that I am seeing you..."*

JINEN: *"He may be bluffing ... What do you suggest?"*

ZARINA: *"May be I should phone him ... he has a sweet corner for me..."*

JINEN: *"Oh, No ... that's not permitted ... you belong to me and no one else ... We have 48 hours until love for eternity..."*

ZARINA: *"What am I going to do with you, my love, let me see if we can stall him for time? ... if I phone him and be nice..."*

JINEN: *"Please do what you think is the best ... and keep in touch with me. It is just a matter of two days!"*

ZARINA: *"I know ... I know ... I feel so happy, my loved one...'*

Part 15

SCENE: Dr. Rajiv Gandhi's residence. Midnight a darkly shrouded stranger is seen ringing the doorbell. Dr. Gandhi is reading in his study den. He looks up surprised and then walks to the entrance door. He looks through the keyhole. Face of horrible disfigured, badly burned, scared face, with the hair on the forehead burned to the roots; white scarf covers the strangers' face. All that can be seen is his piercing blood-shot red eyes, his lips whimpering in pain.

DR. GANDHI: (Puzzled voice commanding an answer before he decides to open the door) *"May I ask ... who is there? Who is it? What is ... Who is it you want to see?"*

STRANGER/DHIRAJLAL: (Stammers in pain) *"I want to see you ... Dr. Gandhi, this is ... your friend ... old friend..."*

DR. GANDHI: *"Who? Please repeat your name? Dhirajlal."*

DHIRAJLAL: (Finding it hard to speak...) *"Dr. Gandhi ... can't you recognize my voice ... Dhirajlal Sheth?"*

DR. GANDHI: (Stands still at the closed door looking more confused, hesitating to open the door) *"No, I cannot ... Did you say Sheth? But we buried him this morning..."*

DHIRAJLAL: (Stammers in pain ... and frustration) *"Yes ... your ... your old friend ... Dhiraj... bhai"*

DR. GANDHI: (Lifts the latch, opening part of the door ... He stares into the strangers eyes in utter disbelief ... then he notices the man's face is badly burned and disfigured. He keeps staring for a moment) *"Are You A Ghost? ... This is ... No ... How is this possible? ..."*

DHIRAJLAL: (He starts to weep in pain) *"Yes, yes ... it is me ... Please let me in ... I am in great pain ... Will you give me shelter in your house?"*

DR. GANDHI: (Recognizing the voice of his mentor and friend) *"Yes, yes ... of course, do come in ... my friend..."*

DHIRAJLAL: *"Please forgive me ... I have been walking for hours ... in a daze ... and I have no where else to go ... at this late hour..."*

DR. GANDHI: (Stands in disbelief staring at the badly burned face, then looking deeply into the sparkling eyes of his friend) *"I thought you were dead ... You are dead ... we cremated you this morning with your wife's remains"*

DHIRAJLAL: *"Well, my friend, I stand before you ... feeling as a dead burned corpse ... resurrected from fire to ashes..."*

DR. GANDHI: (He takes Dhirajlal into his study) *"It is only those eyes that tell me who you are ... You must be in such agony and pain"*

DHIRAJLAL: *"Do not mention pain ... I completely lost my mind ... walking ... deliriously, unable to remember who I was*

... where I am ... until I remembered you ... and walked all the way from the highway ... people screaming when they saw my face..."

DR. GANDHI: (He starts to examine his friend's face)*"Thank god, loosing your memory will have something to do with shock and your badly burned face ... Your skin is all charred deep and dark ... we thought the male body of a man charred black to his bones next to your wife? We identified that body as you..."*

DHIRAJLAL: *"I can explain ... but I desperately need a glass of water ... Where is Mrs. Gandhi?"*

DR. GANDHI: *"She is not here ... she is so upset weeping and asking God why ... about your wife's terrible car accident, she went to stay at her sister-in-law ... her brother's house ... Sit down ... Rest ...*(He pours water from the flask into the silver glass on his desk) *Drink a glass of water ... Tell me what happened"*

DHIRAJLAL: (Drinks the water with much difficulty as his lips are burned and charred ... He take the glass up and pours the water down his throat, without touching his lips...)

"After you explained that Jinen had run away from the hospital, Sharda rushed me to hurry ... in case he had gone home. She was crying and I was steaming with anger, unable to understand why Jinen was causing his mother so much heartache and pain ... I was fuming..."

FLASH BACK

SCENE CHANGE - Jinen's parents are seen driving out of the hospital in the car. As Dhirajlal Sheth stopped at the gate to take a right turn, a stranger the same age of Sheth stands in front of the car, signaling a stop sign with his hands then with a Nameste sign (hitchhiking). There is a screeching of the car breaks to halt, as the man is hit. Dhirajlal rushes out of the car to help the man who lies on the ground, in pain.

DHIRAJLAL: *"Oh, my God, why did you stand in front of the car? Are you hurt? Consider yourself lucky ... I could have ran over you."*

JAGATSINGH/ (ILLIEGAL ALIEN): (Trying to get up with difficulty)*"Please, I am sorry, but I have to run ... oh, my god, I have hurt my foot ... knees ... I cannot walk..."*

DHIRAJLAL: *"Then, get into the car, we are holding up the traffic ... hurry..."*

JAGATSINGH: *"Sahibji (Sir), please turn right quickly and take the main road to the railway station ... so I can avoid ... getting caught..."*

SHARDA: *"Are you in some kind of trouble? What is it ... are you from India?"*

JAGATSINGH: *"Yes, from Punjab (One of the State of India)"*

DHIRAJLAL: *"What is your name?"*

JAGATSINGH:*"I am called Jagatsingh, and I was working as a cook for a family..."*

DHIRAJLAL: *"So what's your story?"*

SHARDA: *"There are some plain-clothes people looking for you on the other side of the road?"*

JAGATSINGH: (He ducks inside the car...)*"Oh, God, please do not let them catch me..."*

DHIRAJLAL: *"Oh, my God, if they catch you ... we will all be in trouble for sheltering an illegal immigrant. That is what you are?"*

JAGATSINGH: *"Please sir, please do not hand me over to the police ... I am not a criminal ... I have done nothing except worked for a family in their home..."*

SHARDA: *"Which family were you working for?"*

JAGATSINGH: *"I was brought by the Chopra family, but they never got my working papers - That was ten years ago ... Now, I am a fugitive working in different places, without working papers..."*

DHIRAJLAL: *"As long as you have not robbed or killed anyone ... Or not a wanted criminal..."*

JAGATSINGH: *"Please sir, on the honor of my mother and father, I have harmed no one ... All I ask that you drop me at the railway station ... and I will be out of your hands"*

SHARDA: *"But why are you so scared?"*

JAGATSINGH: *"The people chasing me are immigration..."*

SHARDA: (She turns to Dhirajlal and pleads)*"He is one of us. They will only deport him ... and he must have reasons for working here to support his family back home..."*

DHIRAJLAL: *"Sharda, have you forgotten we have to get home in case your Jinen is there..."*

SHARDA: *"Yes, yes, I know, but if you take the highway, the railway station is only five minutes from here ... We can drop Jagatsingh off..."*

DHIRAJLAL: *"Okay ... okay ... thank my wife ... she is always helping people ... Your karma is good today..."*

JAGATSINGH:*"I never stole anything ... anything in my life..."*

SHARDA: *"Where will you go?"*

JAGATSINGH: *"I have a friend in Queens who will be able to help me..."*

DHIRAJLAL: *"I suggest that you ask your friend to help you find an immigration lawyer. Having lived here for ten years, you may have some immunity ... try and make it legal, so you can stay in this country and work..."*

JAGATSINGH: *"That has been my dream for the past ten years ... My last employer owned the 7-11 stores, open 24-hours and I was doing many odd jobs, but one of my co-workers found out and notified the immigration officer ... And I had to run and leave everything unfinished ... I cannot afford to get caught. My family needs the money back home."*

DHIRAJLAL: *"Yes, you are correct ... our own people refuse to help ... I am afraid one is ready to help."*

JAGATSINGH: *"Everybody wants to take full advantage of my position, exploiting and paying even below the minimum wages, or not pay me at all, once they find out I am not here with legal papers. What has become of us in this country? ... I have worked in large homes, restaurants, grocery shops, newspaper stands ... no one cares..."*

DHIRAJLAL: *"It is really sad ... People are the same everywhere ... taking full advantage of those in need."*

JAGATSINGH: *"They enjoy squeezing the last drop of blood ... every working hour while we suffer in silence with no choices ... no alternatives"*

SCENE CHANGES One moment the Dhirajlal shifts to third gear the car roars onto the highway while a large truck carrying petrol appears from no where. There is a crashing sound, screeching of car/truck brakes. Flames blaze rising up into the sky with special effects.

DHIRAJLAL: *"It was a nightmare ...this car accident ... I heard a loud blast ... then I was thrown out of the car ... I lay in the bushes ... I must have been unconscious for hours, and when I woke up, it was quiet with the buzzing of cars speeding on the highway above me ... I noticed the street lights ... Somehow, I dragged myself home ... first thing I switched on was the TV which announced the news of our mid-day car accident with the truck carrying petrol (gasoline) ... and photographs of my wife and myself ... I could not believe it ..."*

DR. GANDHI: *"Please ... you must rest ... your burns must be checked out ... otherwise they will become septic ... and you will suffer more..."*

DHIRAJLAL: *"I must have lost conscious. When I woke up again, I had no idea what I was doing ... I took all the cash from my home safe ... the second family car was in the garage ... I could not sleep ... I was in too much pain ...I phoned Siddhi Challum, where I heard the recording announcing the cremation funeral arrangement in the morning..."*

DR. GANDHI: *"Where were you ... you must have felt like a ghost watching his own funeral...?"*

DHIRAJLAL: *"You won't believe it ... I was there ... watching Jinen perform the funeral rites, with you next to him.* (Pause) *I did not know what to do ... there were so many of our friends, all my wife's lady friends weeping ... I was in shock ... and I just stood in the back ... in a distant..."*

DR. GANDHI: *"If I only knew ... If I had looked around ... but we were devastated with the news..."*

DHIRAJLAL: *"How could you know? How could anyone know?'*

DR. GANDHI: *"You must have left the house, just moments before Jinen was there ... He will be so glad to know that you are alive."*

DHIRAJLAL: (Talking as through in a dream not listening to Dr. Gandhi)*"All of a sudden, I began feeling terrible pain and realized that I had become very self-conscious about my* *charred burned face, so I started driving aimlessly ... trying to remember your name and address ... And here I am"*

DR. GANDHI: (He repeated himself)*"Jinen will be so glad to know ... and see you ... his father is alive..."*

DHIRAJLAL: *"Dr. Rajiv, Jinen must not know I am alive..."*

DR. GANDHI: *"Why, I don't understand ... He is your son ...You can share your grief ... He lost his young wife and you've lost Shardaben..."*

DHIRAJLAL: *"I can never share his grief ... This is not the proper time to disclose the truth..."*

DR. GANDHI: *"Never share his grief? What are you talking about, my friend ...Not the proper time..."*

DHIRAJLAL: *"My friend, I cannot explain anything ... I cannot let him know I am alive ... I will explain at the right time. Please understand.* (Pause) *I need you to work on my face. Can you do something ... I am still in agony ... I have been taking pain killing pills from my medicine closet ... but I need your help."*

DR. GANDHI: (Silent ... Starts to examine Sheth's burned charred face ... He opens his first aid kit, cleaning Sheth's face, forehead and neck with ointment) *"I am cleaning your face and I will have to give you some real pain killing medicine. You are in a very bad shape ... You will need plastic surgery ... at least two to three ... skin transplantation treatment ... then time to heal your skin..."*

DHIRAJLAL: *"Can you handle the surgery yourself?"*

DR. GANDHI: *"Yes, yes, of course, but we will have to notify the police that you are alive..."*

DHIRAJLAL: *"My friend ... you are not listening to me ... I am legally dead right now and I want to keep it that way ... No one must know the truth..."*

DR. GANDHI: *"Dhirajbhai, I am very confused ... Why do you not want anyone to know you are alive? You are not a criminal you had an explosive car crash and survived. It is very simple."*

DHIRAJLAL: (In a commanding voice) *"I told you once and I told you twice ...No one must know I am alive ...Please do not unveil my existence ...The truth must not be told ...I need some time to think"*

DR. GANDHI: *"Why are you doing this insane act? Think of the people who love you ... Jinen ... your friends ... your business associates..."*

DHIRAJLAL: *"Please listen ... You must trust me ... I have my reasons. I have never asked you for any favors ... I need this one favor from you, Promise?"*

DR. GANDHI: *"I realize how much you have helped me in the past ... since I came to this country, interned in hospital and then started my medical practice ... I am completely obligated to you ... you have been my greatest mentor ... you are like a father to me..."*

DHIRAJLAL: *"I am not asking for any special favors in payment for what I have done in the past. I am requesting you not to disclose my identity ... until I can decide the right moment..."*

DR. GANDHI: *"How can I perform surgery on your face, neck and forehead, without officially admitting you in the hospital?"*

DHIRAJLAL: *"I request you to admit me under an assumed name like a John Doe ... You understand? Nobody must know who I am..."*

DR. GANDHI: *"Yes, that could be possible ... but life could be simpler..."*

DHIRAJLAL: *"Oh, yes, I am carrying a great deal of money, which I cleaned out of the safe at home. I will not be able to get anything from the bank account ...if I am dead."*

DR. GANDHI: *"Please don't worry about the financial billing ... I can handle it, especially after all you have done for me and my family. You really have no idea how much I am in debt to you ... I will handle all the hospital bills, especially as I am the President of the medical staff in my hospital. That is the least of our problems."*

DHIRAJLAL: *"I knew you are my only hope ... in the help I needed..."*

DR. GANDHI: *"Surgery will change your face completely, as your skin burns are deep. Nobody will recognize you."*

DHIRAJLAL: *"That will be perfect for my plans..."*

DR. GANDHI: *"I simply cannot understand why you are insisting to remain cremated and dead ... Are you loosing your mind?"*

DHIRAJLAL: *"With all that has happened in the last few days ... I wish I could go crazy ... with my wife Sharda gone, but God Mahavirji has kept me alive for his own reasons, I crave a chance to repent and seek forgiveness ... in time."*

DR. GANDHI: *"Repent? Forgiveness?"*

DHIRAJLAL: *"Repent ... for my wife's death ... for beautiful Zarina ... Jagatsingh who took my place with his death ... It is my evil karma that caused all this to happen. I honestly feel I am being given a second chance ...to repent ... and seek forgiveness and the blessings of God Mahavirji..."*

DR. GANDHI: *"So you need time ... to repent and seek forgiveness?"*

DHIRAJLAL: *"Thank you for understanding my friend, but I will need your loyalty and help at times ...that is all I ask ... time..."*

DR. GANDHI: *"You realize this request places me in an awkward position as a professional doctor?"*

DHIRAJLAL: *"Yes, my friend, I am aware of what I am putting you through - but I have no alternative. Please understand I will leave you in peace after the surgery. As if I was never here. Remember you cremated me with my wife ... I am dead..."*

DR. GANDHI: *"Please do not talk like this ... I am so happy to see you alive ... after the heavy grieving sensations at the cremation rites ...It was so overwhelming..."*

DHIRAJLAL: *"Rajiv... today you have proved, without any doubt, you are a great friend ... We will always be true friends - nothing will ever change the friendship we share ... I need to rest ... my head is throbbing..."*

DR. GANDHI: *"Why don't you sleep in the guest room ... You need rest before the surgery ...In the morning I will prepare the paper work and have you admitted..."*

SCENE - Dr. Gandhi in his bedroom, he is in his dressing gown as he rests on the bed, lying down staring on the ceiling...

V/O Dr. Rajiv Gandhi, the man: *"What have you done? Have you gone crazy?"*

V/O of Dr. Gandhi's professional conscious: *"How can you jeopardize your integrity as the President ... You can loose your medical license..."*

V/O Dr. Gandhi's, the man: *"What can I do? Dhirajlal is my friend ... He needs my help ... He needs time..."*

V/O of Dr. Gandhi's professional conscious: *"What do you owe him? Nothing ... you studied and created your professional career with hard work ... sacrifices..."*

V/O Dr. Gandhi's, the man: *"He did many favors for me and my wife ... I owe him."*

V/O of Dr. Gandhi's professional conscious: *"You owe him nothing ... Is he a putting a gun to your head and forcing you to help him ... without questioning him?"*

V/O Dr. Gandhi's, the man: *"I know he has given me no explanations ... but I cannot forget how much I owe him. I cannot be selfish"*

V/O of Dr. Gandhi's professional conscious: *"You owe him nothing ... He must give you some explanations ... you are doing something unprofessional and illegal..."*

V/O Dr. Gandhi's the man: *"When I came to this country, I knew nobody, the day we met ... he became my elder brother, treating me like a family member, in his home ... he used his influence to get me admitted into medical school. What I am today is due to his mentorship ... his generosity..."*

V/O of Gandhi's professional conscious: *"That was such a long time ago ... you have repaid him ... Please do what is right ... You are not obligated to him to ruin your medical career...You are making a major mistake at this stage in your professional career ... Think"*

V/O Dr. Gandhi's, the man: *"At this stage, I must decide the right path..."*

V/O of Dr. Gandhi's professional conscious: *"I am warning you ... you are making a big mistake in admitting him into the hospital for surgery ... You must tell the police, Jinen - he is alive..."*

V/O Dr. Gandhi's, the man: *"I am so glad he is alive ... Let me decide for myself ... I know I am doing the right thing."*

SCENE CHANGES - Dr. Gandhi is having tea with his friend Dhirajlal Sheth who is reading the New York Times and the column about the stock market...

DHIRAJLAL: *"Rajiv, you look troubled ... Did you sleep last night?"*

DR. GANDHI: *"Why do you ask?"*

DHIRAJLAL: *"I know you are honest ... a man of integrity ... you must have been plagued with my demands for time to remain dead..."*

DR. GANDHI: *"Yes ... I was fighting with my conscious..."*

DHIRAJLAL: *"I was sure you were hesitant to my suggestions ... so what did your conscious decide?"*

DR. GANDHI: *"I have notified my operational staff that I will be performing surgery on a family member patient and all bills will be paid by me. This will keep the questions of your identity a secret ...for the time requested."*

DHIRAJLAL: *"Thank you my friend, I will never forget what you have done today ... I will be obligated to you for life..."*

DR. GANDHI: *"I have ordered your admittance into the hospital for surgery and it will be done on a cash basis, which attracts less attention to all the paper work of Medicare, insurance's, etc."*

DHIRAJLAL: *"I hope your decision will not cost your job and put you in jeopardy as the President?"*

DR. GANDHI: *"Let me handle my decision when we come to it..."*

DHIRAJLAL: *"From this day forward, I owe you my life and this worldly existence ... My future for repentance and seeking forgiveness is in your hands..."*

Both men stand up and walk out of the white door and the surgery sign is shown.

FLASH BACK

Part 16

SCENE - Jinen is dressed in a white tuxedo and bow tie. Zarina is dressed in a gown, in a very traditional style. Kevin is dressed in a black tuxedo and bow tie, as the best man. Martha Smith, his girl friend, is in a long white gown, as the bride's maid.

Radio song playing for two lovers while they are waiting.

Love is lightning
Love is brightening,
Very, very slowly,
Very, very knightly
Wake up soul go fast, have some fun in love
Love has a life to live
Long, long life to live
Just go sweetheart
Move fast, move fast
Do not loose fantastic class
Think for great moments
Love has the strength
Love has the braveness
Love has a long life
Go run fast
Oh dear, make relationships forever
Have a wonderful, pleasant time
Oh my love
Oh my love

REGISTRAR: *"Which one of you couples getting married today?"*

MARTHA: (Nudges Kevin in the side with her elbow - they point fingers towards Zarina and Jinen) (Whispers) "*Wish I was getting married...*" (Louder) "*Those two ... They are the bride and bridegroom...*"

REGISTRAR: *"What about you both?"*

MARTHA: *"We are with them as their witness..."*

KEVIN: *"Once we decide to get married, we will come knocking on your door..."*

REGISTRAR: *"Wise guys! Okay, I need the bride and groom to sign the legal document making them husband and wife..."*

A brief paper signing ceremony

REGISTRAR: *"Congratulations, you may kiss the bride ... You are now husband and wife..."*

Jinen Sheth & Zarina Christian are seen kissing each other in slow motion, with parts of the theme song in high tempo.

Song of love and joy as a man and wife.

Our love is in the village of the heart.
To watch our true love fill up with happiness.
The two lovers are great, sparkling soul.
But I have committed to keep.

KEVIN: (Takes photographs with his digital camera)

MARTHA: *"Hey, Jinen how does it feel kissing Zarina for the first time as your wife? Smile ... this is the happiest day of your life!"*

KEVIN & MARTHA: (Clapping, as Martha throws rose petals over the married couple) *"Hey, guys we did it ... I mean you did ... you are now husband and wife! Happiness..."*

All four youngsters hug each other while Kevin pops open a bottle of MOET Champaign.

JINEN: *"Hey Kev and Martha, we would never have been able to get married, if it hadn't been for you both phoning up. Don't forget to be on time!"*

ZARINA: *"This is the happiest day of my life ... I wish our parents were here..."*

JINEN: *"Zarina, my love, my wife ...don't feel sad. Once the storm dies down ... everyone will come to his or her common sense. I am sure we will be one happy family before long..."*

ZARINA: (Whispers) *"Especially when their grandchild arrives..."*

KEVIN: *"Hey guys, after brunch, we have you both ready for the honeymoon. What did you plan, Jinen? A week in the Bahamas? A honeymoon cruise? This is the USA Man, you marry the woman you love ...I am sure your parents will come around ... You only live life once..."*

MARTHA: *"I am sure they will give you their blessings, especially when they see how happy you guys are..."*

KEVIN: *"Hey, there's the stretch limo across the street ... Let's go..."*

All four walk on the pavement with City Hall as the backdrop, Jinen and Zarina move in front with Kevin and Martha behind them more to right. Kevin waves the driver down of the stretch limo that has the door open. At the end of the block, across the street, on the 4th story, a long-range rifle is being aimed. Close-up - through the binocular, the target is aimed at Jinen's chest, as he walks down the steps to cross the road. The rifle follows him for 5 seconds ...as the shooter presses his finger on the trigger. Zarina suddenly throws her arms around Jinen and the bullet hits her head from the back. Slow motion. Her head falls back, her bouquet of flowers in her hand flies in the air. Jinen's close up face looks shocked, he grabs Zarina in his arms refusing to let her fall on the pavement. There is chaos, screaming, yelling. Eyes strain everywhere wondering who and what beast lay unseen. Zarina is placed into the stretch limo with police sirens or ambulance sirens ...

Scene gradually fades away with the song rising to capture the loss of love.

Song.

Oh God, Why did you do this?
Both deserved to be happy in love
It's a shame to be torn apart from their new life
Just a few minutes ago they were committed to each other,
for better or for worse, for richer or poorer, in sickness and in health until death do them part.
The newlyweds deserved your blessings,
But what is karma?
White brides' gown wounded with bloody shot
Lovers lost their faith
Evil won the Game

Part 17

SCENE in Siddhi Challum in the far corner inside the temple. He is lecturing a disciple and the stranger (in reality his own father with a new face)

JINEN: *"Today, we will speak about the message of forgiveness"* (more appropriate quotations)

Two tough-looking men in their 40's, plain-dressed police detectives, enter the room, looking around suspiciously. Jinen stops speaking, when he sees them. He notices them as strangers and approaches them.

JINEN: *"May I help you ... Are you looking for someone in particular?"*

1ST DETECTIVE/ALEX BORDEN: *"Yes, We are looking for one person in particular. My name is Alex Borden, and this is my partner Jefferson Thomas..."*

2ND DTECTIVE/ JEFFERSON THOMAS: *"Hi ... We are looking for..."*

JINEN: (Repeats his sentence) *"How can I help you?"*

ALEX BORDEN: *"We are looking Mr. Jinen Sheth?"*

JINEN: *"Then you have found him ... I was named Jinen Sheth ... before I took the vows to become a Jain monk..."*

JEFFERSON THOMAS: *"Sorry for any interference. We need to talk to you in private..."*

JINEN: *"Yes, yes ... of course ... There is no one here who will disturb your inquiry ... These two men are my disciples ... there is nothing to hide..."*

ALEX BORDEN: (He turns to Jefferson Thomas and makes a grimace, both men shrug their shoulders) *"We have been working on a murder case for some years now ... and have arrested a suspect ... He is in custody...*

JINEN: (Looking confused while his two disciples stand behind him, as though for protection) *"Suspect? But we registered no complaints..."*

JEFFERSON THOMAS: *"Mr. Jinen, we have been working on a murder case for a long time ... you must be aware of it?"*

JINEN: (Nods his head...) *"Yes, yes ... now I remember ... I understand what you are talking about ... but I no longer seek revenge ... I do not want to know anything about finding a suspect ... All the bitterness towards the murderer has passed ... I no longer seek any kind of revenge ... but forgiveness.... There is no more hatred in my heart..."*

THOMAS: *"Don't forget - It was a senseless murder ... we respect your noble thoughts, but we have been working on this particular unsolved murder case for a long time. It has followed all the procedures of law and order ... and the murderer had to be brought to justice, regardless any personal feelings and career changes..."*

JINEN: *"I understand fully ... I am here to cooperate with you, officers."*

ALEX: *"Thanks for understanding our duty ... we appreciate your cooperation."*

JINEN: (He looks at his two disciples, the facial expression of the older man changes, as he moves closer)

DISCIPLE: (Interrupting the conversation) *"Who is ... What is the name of the suspect?"*

ALEX: *"Have you ever heard of a young man called Mustak?"*

JINEN: *"Come again ... That name sounds very familiar..."*

ALEX: *"I repeat Mustak? He was the victim's cousin..."*

JINEN: (A look of surprise on his face, trying to remember where he had heard the name) *"Mustak? Are you sure?"*

THOMAS: *"We are sure. We have the evidence at the police headquarters. We found the murder weapon with his fingerprints on the gun - He is under arrest at the police station."*

JINEN: *"Are you sure? I remember Zarina once mentioned the name ... Mustak ... he was like a family member ... a first cousin ... Why did he commit such a senseless crime? Are you sure?"*

THOMAS & BORDEN: (Both men answer affirmatively together, in one voice) *"We are absolutely sure he committed the crime ... there is no doubt about it ... He has confessed..."*

JINEN: *"With that kind of evidence, you have everything you need. Why do you want me to come down to the police station? I will be of no use to you ... I never met the man."*

ALEX: *"In that case, we need you to confront him as a stranger..."*

JINEN: *"Confront him ... My coming with you both will be of absolutely no help. I never heard the name and so I do not know him. That day ... I never saw the shooter. So I am not a good witness ... I will be of no use to you gentlemen."*

ALEX: *"We have been requested by the arresting officer to bring you in ... We are not asking you to identify him. If you accompany us, you will understand the whole situation. It is very important that you accompany us to the Police Station..."*

JINEN: *"If you insist officers, but I am positive I will be of no help in this case ... I know nothing ... But you must have your reasons ... Come..."*

The three men start walking outside the temple...

JINEN: *"Please give me a few minutes to get ready for the outside world..."*

JEFFERSON THOMAS & ALEX BORDEN (Nodding their heads ... they walk away) *"We will wait for you outside in the unmarked police car..."*

DISCIPLE: (Jinen's father unrecognized plastic surgery) *"Guruji ... May I accompany you?"*

JINEN: *"It is not necessary ... Why take the trouble to go to the Police Station. It may take hours to complete all the paper work formalities..."*

DISCIPLE: (Voice sounds pleading) *"Together we may be of help to each other..."*

JINEN: *"Do you really think so ... They already have the suspect in custody ... what more would they ask?"*

DISCIPLE: *"But two heads are better than one ... It may also be important that I am there with you ... Now I feel I must accompany you, please..."*

JINEN: *"I thank you for your concerns. If you insist I cannot say no. But I do not want you to waste precious time..."*

DISCIPLE: *"It seems like time catches up with one's destiny..."*

JINEN: *"Come; let 's go together after we change for the outside world..."*

Jinen and his father are next seen walking, then sitting inside at the back in the detective's van.

JINEN: (Full face) *"Detectives, I still feel this journey will be a waste of everybody's time..."*

ALEX: (Stares at Jinen suspiciously) *"That may be your opinion ... but bringing you into the Police Station came from our high command ... the Police Commissioner"*

JINEN: *"Yes, we all have to obey the callings of the person who's high in command ... I understand fully..."*

JEFFERSON: (Watching Jinen from the car mirror, while he is driving) *"That is the suspicious part ... Our High Command has ordered us to bring you to the Police Station ... It seems that the murderer is demanding your presence, before he can cooperate fully with the police..."*

JINEN: *"But I have never met the man ... Why does he want to talk to me?"*

JEFFERSON: *"We are very curious. That is the reason, you have got everyone at the Police station suspicious ... It is the murderer's request. He demanded it."*

JINEN: *"I wonder what are his reasons? What could he tell me that would lighten his confession?"*

ALEX & JEFFERSON: *"It took over one week of hard interrogation's ... We wish we knew the answers ... He has refused to say one more word, until you stand before him."*

DHIRAJLAL/DISCIPLE: *"Why ... You both told us in the temple that the police has all the evidence ... What more do you want with our Guruji?"*

JEFFERSON: *"Yes, yes we do have his confession ... with the murder weapon and matching bullets, fingerprints, etc., but for some unknown reasons, he wants to confront you..".*

JINEN: *"Strange ... All this does not make sense ... even after all the evidence and confession..."*

DHIRAJLAL/DISCIPLE: "*This stranger, than reality, why you?"*

JEFFERSON: *"Well, you men speak of forgiveness and peace ... Maybe he wants to confront you for your forgiveness?"*

JINEN: *"Officer ... I have forgiven the murderer a long time ago ... in my search for inner peace through spirituality...*

ALEX: *"Maybe, he wants to confess and tell you why ... what motivated him to murderZarina..."*

JINEN: *"How can I convince you both men ... I have no desire to know earthly realities, which are all part of bad karma..."*

JEFFERSON: *"Nothing is in our hands ... we obey to high authorities."*

JINEN: *"Gentlemen, everything is in our own hands ... how we live life and how we prepare to die..."*

ALEX: *"Our book of law say: You commit the crime by breaking the law, you must pay the price and be punished ... it is the law of the land..."*

JINEN: *"You are correct in that assumption ... But what about kindness - the art of forgiveness ... after his judgement in court, will you set him free?"*

ALEX: *"We appreciate your concerns about our criminal justice. We have done our duty where the justice system will decide the criminal's punishment, after he is found guilty of murder..".*

JINEN: *Yes, yes.. I agree ... But it is sad ... There is no reason to waste another life..."*

JEFFERSON: *"We really know he is the murderer ... Aren't you glad that we caught him ... Why do you want him to go free?"*

JINEN: *"I have nothing to gain from it now. I seek no revenge. I beg your pardon ... I did not mean any harm ... At times, these kinds of murders become no more than news stories for the media to sale their products and news."*

ALEX: *"What about finding justice for the victim and her family?"*

JINEN: *"I am just speaking for myself as a spiritual man. Taking the life of the murderer is not going to bring back the victim. I am not here to judge her family's need for justice ... I have learned to forgive the murderer; it no longer matters whoever he was. All these months, I learned to follow the teachings of God Mahavirji in training to become a monk ... forgiveness and peace are the lifeline of my Jain religion..."*

ALEX: *"Are you a Buddhist? I have never heard of the Jain religion ... We are taught to respect the philosophies of other religions, but American society has its own rules and laws governing its citizens..."*

JINEN: *"Yes, I am aware ... I was born and raised in this country ... but today I should do my spiritual duty, while you both handle law and order..."*

ALEX: *"Well replied, we are all law abiding citizens and must fulfill our duties and obligations to society..."*

DHIRAJLAL/DISCIPLE: (He interrupts the conversation) *"We have been driving for over one hour..."*

JEFFERSON: *"We will reach the Police Station in about five minutes."*

JINEN: (Turns to his disciple) *" I told you to stay behind..."*

DHIRAJLAL/DISCIPLE: *"I am not complaining, but just inquiring when this journey will be over ... I am grateful to be accompanying you..."*

JINEN: *"I am grateful too ... entering the outside world can be rather daunting, when we have not left the Ashram for over one year ... There is so much confusion, doubt and oppression ... I am sorry to be so abrupt with you, I hope I did not hurt you in my speech..."*

DHIRAJLAL/DISCIPLE: *"Hurt? ... You have no idea who will hurt who ... and the devastation ahead..."*

JINEN: *"Those words have awoken my spirit ... Are you trying to tell me something I do not know?"*

DHIRAJLAL/DISCIPLE: (His eyes filled with tears) *"For so long ... I have been trying to gather my courage ... but weakened ... The innocent can no longer be punished for the guilty..."*

JINEN: (Takes his father's hand, patting it softly) *"You are right ... but the man is still only a suspect. In the court of law he has not been sentenced for his guilt. Maybe, he may tell me some truth which will throw light on his innocence..."*

DHIRAJLAL/DISCIPLE: *"I am praying, that will be the case..."*

JEFFERSON: (Breaks the car and opens the door. All four men entered the Police Station) *"Well, gentlemen - we have arrived..."*

NEXT SCENE-Jinen and his father enter the prison cell where Mustak is standing, watching the two strangers.

JINEN: *"You ... you may look familiar? Have we met before?"*

MUSTAK: *"Officers, who are these monks? Why did you bring these holy men here? I don't want to see them…"*

ALEX: *"But I thought you asked to see Jinen Sheth?"*

MUSTAK: (He stares at Jinen carefully...) *"You look a bit like him, especially those eyes ... But why the shaven head? The half starved ... thinner you"*

THOMAS: *"So you do know this monk?"*

MUSTAK: *"I think so. We met on and off ... a long time ago... glimpse at some coffee places, cinema hall ... like it was yesterday ... He accompanied Zarina everywhere?"*

JINEN: *"Yes ... I think I remember you ... you always greeted her with quick smile and a nod ... And ... she did mention you..."*

ALEX: *"So you agree this is Jinen?"*

JINEN: *"You must be Mustak? The officers mentioned your name ... I was told you wanted to meet me..."*

MUSTAK: (Shaking his head, his hands in his hair in desperation) *"I don't believe this ... I can't believe it ... You're a monk?"*

JINEN: *"It is not that difficult to take the vows of a monk..."*

MUSTAK: *"So you are Jinen who became a monk after the murder of his beloved ... the greatest love of his life ... Zarina?"*

JINEN: *"I stand here in judgement..."*

MUSTAK: *"How does it feel to see the face of her killer? You must be very happy to see me captured at last?"*

JINEN: *"There is only forgiveness in my heart ... and my inner soul..."*

MUSTAK: *"How can you forgive me for taking the life of your most precious love...?"*

JINEN: *"It was all part of our karma ... nothing could have stopped the process ... it was the way of life..."*

MUSTAK: *"Aren't you a bit curious? Why I did this horrendous crime? Who was behind the whole master plan?"*

JINEN: *"I no longer judge the actions of others in this life ... I have made peace and received forgiveness for my past life..."*

DISCIPLE/DHIRAJLAL: *"Son, I think we should listen to what he has to confess..."*

JINEN: (Turns to his disciple, nodding his head.) *"Why must we dwell in the past ... a life style which lies dead and buried ... I have no more interest to enter and touch memories of the past ...my spiritual awakening as a monk has no will to return to the thought of it..."*

DISCIPLE / DHIRAJLAL: *"The past is what makes you the man you are ... in this present spiritual life..."*

JINEN: *"My companion, I have no desire to hear his confession ... it will mean nothing to my life now..."*

MUSTAK: *"You must hear the truth..."*

JINEN: *"Will your truth uplift my spirit? ... Or will it simply drag me down to those agonizing depths of human sorrow once again?"*

THOMAS: *"Please, Sir, we need your cooperation. As a good citizen of this country, it is your duty to know the truth..."*

JINEN: *"Detective Thomas, you are placing me in a very dubious position where the purification of my soul will be..."*

ALEX: (Voice his aggravation at Jinen) *"Please, we need this man to tell us the whole truth, and nothing but the truth - so help us God! We have been working on this case for weeks, months and over the years!"*

MUSTAK: (Staring angrily at Jinen's self righteous composure) *"What about my soul? Have I not suffered enough for all the guilty feelings? I too loved Zarina ... since she was a young girl ... we grew up together ... I protected her ... I adored her ... And then she met you ... and for her, there was no one* *else, only YOU ... Can you image my disgust, my hatred for you? ... You stole the only love I had."*

JINEN: (Stunned at this dramatic exposure of his past) *"Please, I realize your suffering ... I forgive you ... Zarina forgives you..."*

MUSTAK: *"Forgive me? I want nobody's forgiveness ... I want all this guilty feeling out of my system ... I want all my nightmares to calm down ... I want my spirit to live in peace ... But the story I have to tell will be mind-blowing to your ears..."*

JINEN: *"I have no fear ... let me help you ease your pain..."*

MUSTAK: (Bursting into crying anger) *"For the record, I never had any intentions ever ... of blindly shooting ... killing ... murdering my beloved Zarina ... I loved her. At the thought of you loving her and she loving you ... it outraged me with jealousy."* (PAUSE ... He rambles in his words hysterically) *"All I wanted was ... to kill you ... You Jinen ... even if it meant with my bare hands! You took her away from me ... I wanted to marry her ... But then I met your father, a case of destiny answer to my problems ... It was your father who came to me and ordered me to remove her from you."*

JINEN: "*Oh, no, no...I don't believe this"*

MUSTAK: *"Next day, I'm watching you both happily married at the door steps of City Hall ... I wanted my revenge ... the bullet was meant for you. Not for my beloved Zarina..".*

Replay the scene of the shooting at City Hall with the beautiful Zarina taking the shot in slow motion

JEFFERSON: *"Who are you accusing? The father was behind the murder plot?"*

MUSTAK: (Nodding his head) *"For months, I tried finding you Jinen, and then reading the papers about your father's car crash - Filled with guilty nightmare, I went into hiding. Then my parents found me and put me into rehab ... and."*

ALEX: *"Drug Rehab ... car crash...? All this time wasted ... in finding the killer..."*

DHIRAJLAL/DISCIPLE: *"He speaks the truth ... I paid this man money to remove her from you, not to kill her..."* (He turns to Jinen) *"This is my karma... I am not worthy of your forgiveness..."*

Camera moves full face into the father's profile. He is led away by the two officers.

JINEN: *"Who am I to pass any judgement on my father? I am a simple monk ... moving on his spiritual journey towards enlightenment..."* (He was looking divine)

PART 18

SCENE: In the temple at Siddhi Challam Jinen is seen praying Jain style before the altar with the three major statues. His eyes are closed and his lips move in quiet tranquillity. There is a calm glow to his face and persona, very spiritual. Deepak Mehta and wife Nicole are seen entering into the Ashram's temple. They wait as Jinen turns, having completed his meditation.

DEEPAK MEHTA AND NICOLE: "*Guruji Jai Jinendra...*"

JINEN: (Turns and sees them) *"Jai Jinendra, Deepak and Nicole ... welcome back ... I am so happy to see you both ... Several times, I have wondered what happened to you ... thank God you both survived the car accident. I felt so responsible ... I have prayed for you all since that time of the accident to ask Mahavirji (GOD) for his forgiveness ... It gives me great pleasure to see you both again at the temple ... God has answered my prayers..."*

DEEPAK: *"Guruji, we have come once more to ask you for your blessings and forgiveness..."*

JINEN: *"You both are blessed ... Your prayers have been answered..."*

NICOLE: (Dressed in a soft traditional Gujarati saree with gold lining befitting a traditional bride) *"Yes ... we have good news ... Deepak's family have accepted me as his wife... All has been forgiven ... we are one happy family..."*

JINEN: *"This is wonderful news ... I am so happy for you both ... God's blessings on your family..."*

Lalbhai and Trishla Mehta enter the temple. Trishla is carrying a baby in her arms they approach Jinen, Deepak and Nicole.

LALBHAI MEHTA: (Glowing with happiness on his face... as he takes the child gently from his wife's arms) *"Swamiji (priest), look, look ... who we have here ... our ... my precious granddaughter ... We are here to ask God Mahavirji's for blessings..."*

JINEN: (He stands and looks at the fair child - a beautiful face with radiance and glow of a mix marriage conception)*"God's blessings on this beautiful baby ... What have you decided to name the child?"*

Lalbhai Mehta places the child in Jinen's arms. Close-up of child smiling radiantly, immediately catches his finger tightly as if he was tied in spiritual recognition refusing to let go (Song starts to play...)

Song.

Hey, what a wonderful moment
Two lovers brought a blossom of joy
Love is blind
Love is a gift from God

True lovers never think about race, religion, or cast
It's Fortunate to fall in love with anyone
Their hearts gave proof of love
Jina is a part of their souls
She's a connection of love
Pray to God,
That he gives them a beautiful life together

TRIASHLA: *"Since my childhood I have loved the name JINA, ... So this beautiful addition to our family ... has been named after Zarina ... Isn't that so beautiful, Jina Mehta? ...* (Pause). *But my daughter-in-law pronounces the name as Jina ... It is a good name for a girl ... especially when she goes to school ... all her school friends will have no problem pronouncing and Remembering her name... Jina... Am I right?"* (Smiling to her grand baby)

JINEN: (Nodding his head ... and repeats the name...) *"Jina ... What a beautiful name for a girl ... she will be greatly loved..."* (Jina means, "STAY ALIVE")

NICOLE & DEEPAK: *"We hope you approve..."*

JINEN: (He walks to the altar with the child in his arms...) *"Let us all God for his blessings and forgiveness for us..."* (Smiling to beloved Jina)

The theme song rises in the midst of this last shot and reaches the heights of the Siddhi Challum landscape outside into the sky and beyond.

Love, forgiveness, repentance, non-violence, devotion, peace. Story of a monk, JINEN, & ZARINA.

Whose love? This is all I think.
Our love is in the village of the heart.
He will not see me stopping here ever.
To watch our true love fill up with happiness.
Our little horse love may think it queer.
To stop without a secret love farmhouse near.
Between two lovers will be the "STORM" of the century.
He gives harness bells shake.
To ask if there is some error.
The only other skies that sweep.
Of stormy wind and downy flake.
The two lovers are great, sparkling soul.
But I have committed to keep.
And miles to fly in ending love.
Before I sleep…
Before I sleep…

In the 20th Century

JIN: "*Good Morning Zari. Hey sweetheart, It's 4 a.m., you know we are going to visit Buddha Gaya (Buddhist Ashram). I love you…*" (Jin is her boy friend. They both kiss each other.)

ZARI: "*Hey, I lost my beautiful dream. Darling, Can we postpone your Bbbb means Buddha Ggggg Gaya today?*" (Mumbling)

JIN: "*Honey, It's very hard to get an appointment again. I think you should email your beautiful dream tomorrow, to my dreamland and no more talk. I would love to discover your happy dream. Come on darling, let's get up. By the way who was in your dream today? Is it me and you and our love life?*"

ZARI: "*Yeah looks like you and me in the 19th century. We were old lovers. I don't know! But you are mine, mine, and mine! In this life, but in my dream I saw you as Jinen and me as Zarina. God knows… O.K. Let's see if we will.*"

They both get ready. While traveling to Ashram Jin is falling asleep.

Zari started to read "Vegetarianism" book

Reasons to be a vegetarian
If you have ever loved an animal
If you believe in non-violence
If you cannot give life, for then you have no right to take life away
If you want to prevent life disease
If you want to prevent cancer
If you want to avoid bacterial contamination
I you have compassion for living beings
If you don't want your pet to end up as cow food when he/she dies
If you want to have inner peace and calm
If you want to save water
If you want to protect the rainforests
If you want to conserve energy
If you want to help the hungry
If you want to help poverty
If you want to eat sattvic food (meat is not sattvic)
If you want to prevent diabetes
If you want to prevent strokes
If you want to prevent constipation and other bowel diseases
If you want to live longer
If you want to live an honest life
If you want to feel less aggression, anger or restlessness
If you want to help feed starving children

If you want to have healthy digestive tract
If you want to live a spiritual life
If you want to be a Yogi
If you want lower your cholesterol
If you want to lower your blood pressure
If you want to loose weight
If you want to live in accordance with human's natural systems
If you want to make fullest of our human birth
If you have compassion
If you think it is wrong to cause pain conscious, feeling creatures, if you have mercy
If you want to take a stand for the environment
If you don't want to financially support the factory farmers who tortures animals
If you want your body to be true pure temple for god
If you do not want to make your body a graveyard.
Jai Ho, Jai Ho, Jai Ho
Jai Jai Jai Ho...

Zari is continuing book...

The End

About Author

Hansa M. Shah, R.N. My first Novel, Movie Drama Book "STORM JIN-ZARI". Unfortunately, Chloe production Films LLC postponed this project due to financial crisis. This story came in my heart because I missed my youngest great brother Pradeep. Deep left us. At last I urge all the amazing people and all novel readers, to enjoy this fiction story. May God Bless and fulfill my dream. Life is full of love for every creature, if they have an understanding soul.

CHARACTERS: (IN ORDER OF APPEARANCES)

1. Zarina- 24 years old, 5'5" height, fair skinned, thin, black hair, and big dark brown eyes. Very beautiful and pleasant girl. Indo-American. She works as financial consultant in Wall Street. Mother is Muslim and father is Christian.
2. Jinen-26 years old, 5'9" height, fair skinned, muscular body, with mustache, black hair, and black eyes. Handsome and intelligent man. Indo-American. He works in a financial stock market at Wall Street. Parents are Jain.
3. Deepak-25 years old. Indo-American Jain boy. Black hair, black eyes, handsome, thin and a sweet boy. Parents are diamond merchant. He is a MBA student.
4. Nicole-21 years old. American girl, Christian. A college student. Kind and an innocent pretty girl.
5. Lalbhai Mehta-50-years old, 5'10 height. Indo-American, business man. Diamond merchant. (Father of Deepak)
6. Trishla- 45 years old, 5'5" height, fair skinned and thin. Indo-American women. (Deepak's Mom)
7. Sharda- 48 years old, 5'6" height, Indo-American woman. (Jinen's Mom)
8. Dhirajlal-54 years old, 5'8" height. Handsome, mustache, fair skinned and healthy. (Jinen's Father)

9. Manglaben-74 years old, 5' height, typical American Indian. (Jinen's Grandmother)
10. Dr. Rajiv Gandhi-50 years old, 5'8" height. Popular dedicated plastic surgeon. (Friend of Dhirajlal)
11. Kevin-26 years old, 5'6" height. American Christian. Gentle, kind and intelligent. Finance MBA student. (Jinen's best friend.)
12. Martha –25 years old, 5'5" height. African American girl. Intelligent and sweet girl.
13. Nurse Florence Knightingile Karla-22 years old, 5'3" height. Charming and attractive American nurse.
14. Chandramohan-55 years old, 5'8" height and thin. Siddhi Ashram monk. Devoted to Jain religion.
15. Mustak-24 years old, 5'"9 height, 160 lbs. A chubby guy, an alcoholic and a Muslim boy.
16. Jagatsingh-54 years old, 5'7 ½ " height. Sing but, not turban. American dressed illegal alien. Worked in a restaurant as a cook struggling to receive his green card. Wanted to settle in USA.
17. Registrar- 37 years old, 5'6" height and overweight about 255 lbs. American Italian. Sweet and friendly.
18. Alex Borden- 35 years old, 5'9" height and 145 lbs. American. Dedicated detective.
19. Jefferson Thomas- 42 years old, 5'8" height and 160 lbs. African America. (Assistant detective Borden)
20. Jina (Infant baby)- 3 months old. Very beautiful and happy baby.
21. Jin-23 years old, 5'8" height. Indo-American, a Buddhist boy. A college student.
22. Zari-21 years old, 5'5: height. American, Christian girl. A college student.

23. Leader- 21 years old, 5'6" height. Wears worn out jeans, Black Jacket. Earring on left ear. Hispanic male.
24. Second guy-19 years old, 5'7" height. African American male.
25. 25. Third guy- 18 years old, 5'6" height. Caucasian male. Earring on right ear.

Treatment

This is a story of a cross-cultural wedding not permissible in the family. A young couple (Jinen and Zarina) gets married against their parents' will, and the wife gets killed mysteriously. Husband (Jinen) becomes a Jain Monk. After years has passed by a young couple comes to him (Deepak and Nicole) in Ashram and asking him for help. A monk dreams about his past. The father (Dhirajlal) remains as a Disciple of the monk (Jinen). After a facial surgery following a car accident for repentance of his guilt. This is a Thrilling story of Love, Suspense, Forgiveness, and Repentance. The story has a few turns and twists. Making readers want to keep reading until the end.

"GOD BLESS"

The End